GHOSTLY AMETHYST SHADOWS

Jennifer J. Morgan

Books by Jennifer J. Morgan

2022 Finalist - American Fiction Awards
Mystery/Suspense and Cozy Mystery (*Shadows in the Forest*)

2024 Winner - International Impact Awards
Best Fiction- Cozy Mystery (*Shadows in Alaska*)

* * *

Libby Madsen Cozy Mysteries

Shadows in the Forest
Spa Shadows
Shadowed Treasures
Shadow Retreats
Spooky Shadows
Shadow's Christmas Wish
Festive Shadows
Shadows in Alaska
Shadows Over Thanksgiving
Ghostly Amethyst Shadows
The Christmas Fairy - a holiday novella

GHOSTLY AMETHYST SHADOWS

Libby Madsen Cozy Mysteries, Book 10

Jennifer J. Morgan

Secret Staircase Books

Ghostly Amethyst Shadows
Published by Secret Staircase Books, an imprint of
Columbine Publishing Group, LLC
PO Box 416, Angel Fire, NM 87710

Book layout and design by Secret Staircase Books
First trade paperback edition: February, 2025
First e-book edition: February, 2025

Publisher's Cataloging-in-Publication Data

Morgan, Jennifer J.
Ghostly Amethyst Shadows / by Jennifer J. Morgan.
p. cm.
ISBN 978-1649142092 (paperback)
ISBN 978-1649142108 (e-book)

1. Libby Madsen (Fictitious character). 2. Romantic suspense—
Fiction. 3. Arizona—Fiction. 4. Amateur sleuths—Fiction. 5. Women
sleuths—Fiction. I. Title

Libby Madsen Cozy Mystery Series : Book 10.
Morgan, Jennifer J., Libby Madsen cozy mysteries.

BISAC : FICTION / Mystery & Detective.

813/.54

Dedication

To my grandmother, who passed away within the past year at the age of 95. She was amazing. The strongest, bravest human being I've known and probably ever will know. We had a close relationship and I was enormously blessed to spend quality time with her for so much of my life.

I once worried about how terribly I'd miss her when she'd gone to Heaven. However, that's not how it's worked out at all. I have felt her with me every single day since. She's never left my side.

I love you, Grandma.

Acknowledgements

Thank you to my editors and beta readers: Lee Ellison, Marcia Koopmann, Susan Gross, Paula Webb, Isobel Tamney, Dawn Hasiotis, Eve Osborne, Gabi Hoffknecht, and Jane Litherland. You catch stuff I stop seeing after so many revisions. I truly appreciate you!

My husband, Doug, and my friends Marcy, Dolores, and Aileen—thank you so much for your continued support! It means the world to me that you have my back.

My four-legged loved ones—past and present—are a constant source of inspiration. Without each one, this series would have never come about. Their personalities and loving companionship continue to keep my creative side going.

And most importantly, thank you to every reader who has ever picked up one of my books. I have received such nice notes from so many of you and I am so inspired by your never-ending support. To think I only started this journey as a published author nearly three years ago is remarkable. It feels like I've gained so many reader friends in such a short time (I have!). Thank you for giving this new author a chance—I'm forever grateful!

CHAPTER ONE

The sun was barely rising and the cool desert air was still clinging to the shadows of the Four Peaks, as they tightened the straps on their backpacks. Greg stood a few feet away, scanning the horizon, his hand brushing over his jacket pocket where a small velvet box rested, hidden from view. He took a deep breath, imagining the moment—the cliffs, the sweeping vistas.

"Ready?" he heard her soft voice call out, as she adjusted Shadow's leash. The black Labrador wagged her tail eagerly, sensing their adventure ahead. Libby slid on her knit hat over her shoulder length auburn hair.

Greg smiled, nodding. "More than ready."

From the campground, they set off on the designated trail, their boots crunching over gravel as they began their ascent into the wilderness. The scent of desert sage and creosote filled the air, mingling with the faint hum of quail skittering about. Other than that, it was quiet, almost too quiet.

"You think we'll find any artifacts out here?" Libby asked, glancing up with a playful grin.

Greg chuckled, but his thoughts were already racing. He'd always heard about Four Peaks Wilderness, but had never hiked the trails. And that's what triggered this excursion. He thought it was the ideal place for the proposal, secluded and also with an air of mystery. He just needed the right moment. Maybe tonight, under the stars, back at their campsite? He hadn't decided yet.

They hiked along easily, but as they continued deeper into the rugged terrain, the trail became narrower, more uneven. The desert scrub thickened, and the wind shifted—carrying with it a faint scent that neither of them could place.

Shadow stopped suddenly, ears pricked, growling low in her throat.

Libby frowned. "What is it, girl?"

Greg squinted into the trees. A strange unease washed over him, though he couldn't explain why. "Probably just a deer," he said, but his voice held the slightest hint of doubt.

Libby shot him a look and shrugged it off, tugging gently on her dog's leash. "Come on. We've got a long way to go."

As they walked on, the morning sun climbed higher, casting golden light over the landscape as they continued their climb. The trail twisted between clusters of boulders and cacti, with Shadow occasionally bounding ahead, nose to the ground.

Greg noticed that the unsettling feeling he had earlier hadn't gone away. Was it that the surroundings seemed quieter than he'd expected? Where were the other hikers who'd spoken so highly of these trails? And what was that faint metallic scent that still lingered in the air? Pushing his thoughts aside, he tried to focus on the trip—and, more importantly, on finding the optimum time to propose.

"So," Libby said, breaking the silence, "how far does the trail go? You said you found something about it online?"

"Yeah," Greg replied, forcing himself to sound casual. "We'll go up on the ridgeline, about two hours from here, I think. Eight miles round trip, at least, I think. I've got the GPS coordinates." He glanced at his watch. "We should get there by early afternoon."

Libby nodded, her eyes scanning the rugged landscape. "This place feels … isolated, you know? I'd have thought there'd be more hikers out here. It's almost as though it's been waiting around for centuries without a soul to discover it."

Greg chuckled. "Yeah, centuries or longer." He hesitated for a moment, then added, "Of course, we know people hike up here in these hills, so we're certainly not the first. You sure you're up for it? It's quite a climb."

"Of course." She grinned, giving him a playful nudge. "I've been looking forward to this hike for weeks. Besides, it's gorgeous out here. And mysterious, don't you think?" she added, her voice teasing.

Greg nodded, and they walked in comfortable silence for a while longer, but as they rounded a bend in the trail, Shadow stopped suddenly again. This time, she froze completely, her body tense, eyes locked on something in the distance. A low growl formed, rumbling in her throat.

Libby tugged her leash, but Shadow wouldn't budge. "What's gotten into her?" she muttered.

Greg followed the dog's gaze and saw it: a figure, far off in the trees, half-hidden by the shadows. Maybe other hikers? Something about the way the person stood—too still, too distant—gave him pause.

"Hey!" Greg called out, raising his hand. "You okay?"

No response. The figure stood motionless.

Libby's brow furrowed as she glanced between her boyfriend and the figure in the distance. "Weird…"

Greg took a step forward, feeling uneasy. "Maybe they're lost? Should we go check?"

But before they could decide, the figure turned sharply and disappeared into the trees, melting into the thick foliage like smoke.

Libby shivered, pulling her jacket tighter around herself. "That was strange."

"Yeah." Greg's pulse quickened. He tried to laugh it off. "Probably just another hiker who didn't want to be bothered." But deep down, he didn't believe it. Something about the whole situation somehow felt wrong.

Continuing along the trail, Greg kept glancing over his shoulder, half-expecting the person to reappear. He was still trying to shake the feeling when they reached a fork in the path.

"Which way?" Libby asked, looking between the two trails, and taking a second to sip some water from her bottle. Both trails seemed narrow and winding, but one led deeper into some scrub, while the other curved upward toward a rocky ridge.

Greg pulled out his phone to check the GPS

coordinates. "This one," he said, pointing toward the trail that led along the rocky ridge. "It should take us to where I was thinking would be a great lookout point."

But as they started down the path, a strange noise echoed from the forest beyond—like metal scraping against rock, faint but unmistakable.

Greg and Libby exchanged glances. "What was that?" she whispered.

Greg's hand automatically went to his pocket, where he had concealed the ring securely, and wishing he had something better suited to protect them. "I don't know," he answered. "But let's keep moving."

As they ventured deeper into the wilderness, the air grew heavier, the pungent scent stronger. And somewhere, just out of sight, the sound of scraping metal continued.

The chilly air became colder as they walked, despite the sun climbing higher overhead. Libby's steps slowed as the sound continued, irregular but persistent, like someone— or something—was working away just beyond the trees, out of their view.

"I don't like this," she muttered, tightening her grip on Shadow's leash. The black Labrador pinned her ears back, her posture tense, as if she was picking up on something that neither human could see. "Are we even supposed to be here?"

Greg swallowed the knot of unease in his throat. "Sure, plenty of people hike these trails. It's probably just the wind exaggerating some camper's activities," he said, but even he didn't believe his own words.

Libby shot him a skeptical look. "Wind? Scraping metal?"

He forced a smile, trying to lighten the mood. "Weren't

there mines in this area—at least at some point in history? Maybe they're still around and working today. I don't know."

She rolled her eyes, with her lips quirked in a half-smile. "I hope not. Or, at least, I hope they do not run us off if there are workers up here."

They pressed on, the path narrowing again as they followed the trail deeper into the woods. The dense canopy of trees blotted out most of the light, casting long shadows across the wilderness. Despite Arizona's temperate winter air, Libby wished she'd brought a warmer jacket. Shadow was still alert, occasionally sniffing the air, her tail low.

Just when the background sounds seemed to settle into something almost manageable, they came upon a clearing—a small, open space surrounded by jagged rocks. The trees were thinner here, and the light filtered through in slanted beams. But what caught their attention was the massive, rusted metal contraption in the center of the clearing.

Libby's breath caught. "Greg, is that—?"

"Old mining equipment, it looks like." Greg crouched beside the wreckage, running his fingers gently over the weathered metal.

It was an old mining cart, tipped on its side, half-buried in the earth. Chains wrapped around its broken wheels, and beside it, someone had discarded a rusted pickaxe in the dirt. A faint shimmer glinted from the surrounding ground—rock fragments, scattered and dull with the dust.

She knelt next to him, picking up a small shard. "This is amazing ... it looks like no one's been here for decades."

Greg stood and scanned the area, nodding his head. "Yeah, I wonder what they mined here? I've read how many of these small operations shut down pretty quickly."

"But who was that person we saw earlier?" she asked, her voice barely a whisper. "If no one's been here for ages … who was that?"

Greg was about to respond when Shadow barked—a loud, sharp sound that echoed through the wilderness. The dog's body tensed, and she pulled at the leash, her nose pointing toward a cluster of rocks at the far end of the clearing.

Libby stood, clearly startled. "What is it, girl?"

Before Greg could react, Libby walked toward the rocks, with Shadow straining on the leash. Greg followed, scanning the area warily. This wasn't how the day was supposed to go. He'd imagined proposing amongst scenic views and perhaps a beautiful sunset, not amid strange noises, smells, and what appeared to be abandoned mines.

As they rounded the boulders, the ground sloped down, leading to a narrow opening in the rock face—a small cave entrance, partially hidden by overgrown brush. The metallic scent was stronger here, and the soft scraping sound echoed from within.

Libby froze. "No way," she whispered, staring at the dark opening in the earth. "That's definitely a mine."

Greg's instincts screamed to turn back, but something about the cave pulled him in, like it held some answers to yet unknown questions.

"Do you think we should check it out?" Greg said, his voice wavered.

Libby, ever the adventurer, advanced closer. "What if this is part of an old mine? What if there's treasure in there?" she asked excitedly.

Greg hesitated, torn between his worry about their

safety and his desire for the perfect hiking adventure. He wanted to explore—but he also didn't want to risk anything happening.

As Libby took another step forward, the ground beneath her shifted. The rocks gave way with a loud *crack*, and before she could react, the earth collapsed beneath her feet. With a yelp, she tumbled several feet into the darkness of the cave, dragging Shadow with her.

"Libby!" Greg shouted, lunging forward just as she disappeared into the void.

He dropped to his knees at the edge of the collapse, peering down into the darkness. Dust and debris filled the air, but he could hear Libby coughing below. Shadow barked frantically, the sound echoing up from the cave.

"Are you okay?" Greg called, his heart pounding.

"I think so." Her voice sounded shaky, but unhurt. "It's not that deep, but … I think I'm going to need help to get back up."

Greg's mind whirred. He'd brought a rope; it was in his pack. "Hang on," he said, fumbling to get his backpack off to retrieve it. "I'll pull you up."

Before he could untangle the rope, a low rumble reverberated through the ground. Greg froze, listening, as the sound grew louder—closer.

"Greg…" she started hesitantly. "Uh, there's something down here."

Greg floundered with the rope, the rumbling beneath the ground making his hands shake. He glanced down into the darkness where Libby had fallen, his flashlight casting a thin beam of light into the void. Shadow's barking had grown more frantic, echoing off the stone walls of the cave.

"Hold on, Libby, I'm coming!" Greg called, trying to keep his voice calm.

"I'm okay, but…" Her voice wavered. "Something's moving down here."

The scraping noise reverberated through the cave again, louder this time, almost rhythmic. It wasn't only the sound of metal—it was like something was being dragged. Greg's skin prickled.

As he tossed the end of the rope down, his mind flashed to all the unsettling things they'd encountered so far—the strange figure in the trees, the metallic scent, the old mining cart, and now this hidden cave. He had thought this trip would be a romantic getaway, but instead it was starting to feel like they'd stumbled into something they weren't meant to find.

"Grab the rope!" Greg shouted, trying to keep the urgency out of his voice.

She grabbed it, wrapping it around her arm and also securing Shadow's leash. As Greg braced himself and pulled, they both heard the scraping getting closer. Greg shuddered to think it could be something, or someone, following Libby and Shadow.

With grunts and groans, Greg provided the leverage for Libby to climb up and over the edge of the collapsed earth. Shadow scrambled up beside her owner, still growling toward the cave.

Greg collapsed back onto the ground, panting, as Libby sat beside him, wiping dirt from her hands. "Thanks," she said, her voice breathless. "But Greg … there's something down there. I saw—"

Before she could finish, a sharp clang echoed from within the cave. They both froze, staring at the dark hole.

The scraping stopped, replaced silence.

"What did you see?" Greg whispered, sitting up, his pulse racing again.

"I'm not sure," she said, shaking her head. "It was dark, but I swear there was a figure ... something hunched over, moving through the tunnel. It had a pickaxe."

Greg stammered. "A person?"

"I don't know. Yes, but also ... well, it wasn't normal human behavior. Its movements were slow, jerky. Like it wasn't alive." Libby shuddered at the memory. "Honestly, kind of ghost-like."

Greg stood up, staring at the cave entrance. "We need to get out of here."

Libby nodded, still shaken. "Agreed."

They hurriedly made their way down the trail, Greg glancing over his shoulder every few steps. His thoughts flitted—who *or what* was in that cave? The logical part of him wanted to write it off as a trick of the light, their overactive imaginations, or maybe an old mining tunnel collapsing, but his gut told him there was more to it than that.

As they hiked, the sun dipped lower in the sky, casting long shadows across the Four Peaks Wilderness. The farther they went, the more they sensed they were being watched. Greg's grip tightened on Libby's hand, and he could feel the box in his jacket pocket again. So much for a romantic proposal. He'd imagined a pure moment shared under the stars, but now, every sound made him feel like they were in danger.

They finally reached a ridge overlooking the valley, a breathtaking view of the Phoenix metro area, bathed in the orange glow of the setting sun. For a time, the beauty of it all made Greg forget the cave and the strange figure they'd seen. This was it—an excellent spot, despite everything. Maybe if they just took a breath, he could salvage the proposal.

"Libby," Greg began, turning to her with a soft smile, "I know today's been … well, really weird. But there's something I've been wanting to—"

A loud crash came from behind them, followed by the sound of rocks tumbling down the trail. Both of them spun around, and there, at the edge of the ridge, was the figure they had seen in the woods earlier.

It was hunched, dressed in old, tattered clothes, its face obscured by shadows, but the pickaxe in its hand gleamed in the dying light. It took a step forward, dragging the tool behind it, the sound of metal against rock echoing through the quiet night.

"Run," Greg urgently whispered, grabbing her arm.

They bolted down the trail, Shadow barking wildly beside them. The figure didn't chase, but Greg could hear the scraping sound, following them like a ghostly echo as they darted through the trails.

They didn't stop running until they were back at their campsite, panting and breathless. Greg's hands shook as he grabbed the tent poles, frantically packing up their gear.

"What *was* that?" Libby asked, her eyes wide with fear. "It—it wasn't human, was it?"

"I don't know," Greg said, his mind spinning. "I can't even imagine what that thing was, but we're not staying to find out."

As they finished packing up their gear, the wind picked up, rustling through the bushes with a haunting whistle. Shadows lengthened, and the vast wilderness seemed to close in around them. The strange scent filled the air once more, and somewhere in the distance, the scraping sound continued.

Greg glanced at Libby; his heart was heavy, sad it hadn't turned out as he wanted. Then he shook it off. They had to leave, though. At least they'd be safe back at home.

As they hurriedly shouldered their packs and started toward their vehicle, the figure in the woods haunted him. Maybe they hadn't just stumbled upon an abandoned mine—*maybe something else had found them.*

CHAPTER TWO

The next morning, after settling in back at home in Mesa, Greg and I shared the unease that still lingered with us from the hike the day before. Over coffee, we agreed it was a great adventure—spooky, but also exhilarating. There was something Greg wasn't saying—I kept thinking that the ghost, or whatever it was, rattled him much more than me.

"Are you still thinking about inviting the gang over for a BBQ?" I asked him. "I'm up for it, if you are."

His gaze held a haunted look. Or I was reading way too much into it. Finally, he visibly shook it off and turned to me.

"Sure. It would be fun to see everyone. We really haven't done anything with them since Thanksgiving, have we?"

I nodded. "That's what I was thinking."

"Mind if I invite a work buddy?"

"Not at all."

By evening, the air was cool, and the patio lights glowed softly over the backyard, casting a relaxed glow over our small group. The outdoor heaters kept everyone comfortable. Greg flipped burgers on the grill while Bella and I set out place settings, chips, dips, and side salads on the table. It was nice catching up with my former roommate, who'd been dying to hear about our hike.

"So," Bella leaned in as I handed her a drink and asked, "how was the big adventure in the mountains?"

I grinned, glancing at Greg. "It was ... intense. The scenery was beautiful—mountain views, sprawling desert. But it was also kind of eerie in places. There was this strange stillness, and we kept feeling like something was ... watching us, *following* us?"

One of Greg's friends from work, Al, raised an eyebrow. "Watching you? Like a mountain lion or something?"

I laughed, though the memory of the shadows and that chill in the cave made my spine tingle. "Not quite. Actually, we both thought we saw a man. But..." I glanced across the patio at Greg, who was smiling but watching me with that look he gets when he knows I'm about to tell a good story.

Greg nodded, then announced, "Burgers are ready. Everyone take a seat at the table and we'll tell you our ghost tales." He chuckled as he loaded the last burger onto the platter and headed to the expansive teak wooden table.

I heard the mumblings of 'ghost tales?' being uttered

as everyone pulled chairs out and got settled at the table.

Al and Bella sat next to each other. I caught Greg glancing sheepishly their way and figured out that was the strategy behind inviting his work buddy. Lexi, JJ, and Joshua found their seats, and Shadow knew to stay under the five-year-old's chair to catch all the falling goodies. This dog was no dummy.

JJ prompted Greg. "So, about this cave you found?"

"Right. Yeah, we stumbled upon it on our hike yesterday, and there was some other strangeness. A man lurking in the woods—only, we're not entirely sure it was actually human. I don't know, but there was this whole aura about it. I know it sounds weird."

Everyone around the table went quiet as Greg told the story, and then Lexi, who'd been listening intently, spoke up. "So, was it actually a cave? Or a mine? Or? It's just strange because I only recently learned that there's supposed to be an old amethyst mine up in Four Peaks somewhere. Maybe you found it?"

Greg and I exchanged glances. "Really? We had no idea about an amethyst mine," I said. "But we came across old mining equipment so that makes sense. Everything we saw was really old and weathered—"

Lexi nodded, looking intrigued. "I think I read about it somewhere—a mining operation from way back. People tell wild stories about miners who got trapped and how the place is supposedly haunted." She leaned in, eyes wide. "You two should look it up. If it is the mine, you might have found something historic!"

Greg chuckled, but there was a spark of curiosity in his eyes. "You know, we might just have to dig a little deeper." We all groaned at his pun. The conversation moved on to other topics, but what Lexi revealed lingered in the back of my mind. What if that cave actually was part of the old amethyst mine?

As we settled into our meal, Bella leaned back in her chair, taking a sip of her drink. "You know, if you guys are up for more adventure, try kayaking at Canyon Lake," she said, her eyes lighting up. "Coves extend far back, with hidden spots everywhere. Very romantic." Her eyebrows wiggled.

Greg's face lit up with interest, and I could almost see the wheels turning. "That sounds like a great idea," he said, shooting me a quick glance.

"Oh, it's amazing," Bella continued. "You can find spots that are so secluded it's like they're all yours. Plus, the views are incredible. Steep cliffs and the wildlife—eagles, bighorn sheep—they're amazing. Just imagine—paddling out early in the morning, sun just coming up. Or, likewise, at sunset ... gorgeous."

Then Al, who'd been listening with a grin, chimed in. "And if you're feeling really bold, you could try cliff diving! You'd be surprised how many teens love jumping off the cliffs there."

I laughed, shaking my head. "I think I'd leave that to the thrill-seekers, but the kayaking part sounds excellent."

Greg nudged me, looking more convinced by the minute. "What do you say, Libby? A day on the water, exploring those coves?"

I could feel his excitement building. "Alright, you've convinced me. Let's make it our next adventure."

Joshua asked with wide eyes, "Can we go cliff diving?"

Both Lexi and JJ answered in unison. "No!"

Laughing, I stood up. "Anyone want another drink?

I'm headed in to get another glass of wine." Trying to keep tabs of the orders shouted in my direction, I opened the sliding door and realized Lexi followed me.

"Hey, I'd be really interested in what you learn about that mine. Maybe we all could do another hike there one day."

A shiver took hold of me. "I'm not certain I actually *want* to return there. Don't get me wrong, the nature was beautiful. But our experience was creepy."

"Well, keep us in mind if you do another hike."

"Will do. Hey, what do you think of that pairing?" I pointed out the door to where Bella was sitting.

Lexi's eyes flew open. "Are you two setting them up?"

I chuckled. "Greg didn't say specifically, but I wondered that myself when I saw them sit down next to each other. They're cute."

"How old is Al, anyway?"

"Oh. I'm not sure."

"Bella's only in her twenties. Please tell me he isn't our age and nearly hitting forty."

I shrugged and handed her several of the beers to carry outside. "I don't think so. At least he seems younger than us. I'm horrible at guessing ages, though."

Later that night, after everyone left, and the backyard was quiet again, I turned to Greg, unable to shake the idea.

"Do you think ... we really could have found that amethyst mine?" I asked, half-joking but curious.

Greg's eyes sparkled in the dim light of the kitchen. "Why? You wanna go back?"

I shot him a look.

"Seriously, there's one way to find out. I'll do a little research and see what I can learn."

* * *

Greg and I both shook off the unusual events from our hike the weekend before, and after an uneventful work week, he was clamoring to get the kayak out on the lake on Saturday.

He'd brought out the tandem kayak from storage, and the plan was simple: paddle to a secluded cove and enjoy a romantic lunch for two. I had packed the wine and a nice charcuterie selection. No cliff diving or risk-taking this weekend—only quiet solitude.

Driving to the boat launch area, I gazed out over the vista. Canyon Lake was stunning—a serene oasis surrounded by steep, rocky cliffs. The water reflected the blue sky with scattered puffy white clouds. It looked to be a quiet day with only a few boats on the water.

As we pushed off from the shore, the afternoon sun glinted off the water. It was a perfectly sunny winter day in Arizona. Warm when we were basking in the sunshine, but yet too cold to go into the water. Each of us, with a paddle in hand, kept a strong stable cadence, and made our way along the perimeter of the lake and over to one of several coves. Cruising along at a fairly good clip, we couldn't help laughing at Shadow. Her ears flapped in the breeze as she lounged on the boat's stern, seemingly eager to see where we were taking her. Greg took a deep breath. His look of contentment made me wonder what was going on in that brain of his. One thing was for sure, something had preoccupied him lately.

"The lake is gorgeous this afternoon," I said, trailing my fingers through the cool water once we slowed for a break. "We need to do this more often. It's so close by and our mild winter weather makes it possible this time of year."

"Yeah," Greg agreed, displaying his thousand-watt smile. "Wait till you see the cove I have in mind. It's even more beautiful."

We paddled in sync again, the quiet rhythm of our strokes filling the air. But as we rounded a bend, everything changed. The wind picked up suddenly, sending ripples across the water. The sky, which had been clear earlier, was now showing signs we could be in for an overcast afternoon, and the temperature dropped just a little too quickly for comfort.

"There wasn't a storm in the forecast, was there?" I muttered, glancing at the sky.

"No," Greg replied, disappointment creeping into his voice.

Before we could decide about turning back, the kayak wobbled, rocked by an unexpected swell. Greg's grip tightened on the paddle as I gasped, my eyes wide, trying to hold Shadow in her precarious position.

"Did you feel that?" I asked. "That was spooky."

My pulse quickened. It wasn't just the wind. The water itself seemed to have shifted beneath us, as if something large had passed below the surface. I shook the thought away—this wasn't the time to let my imagination run wild.

"Let's keep going," Greg said, though his voice sounded less confident than before. "The water will be calmer in the cove."

As we approached the inlet, the wind howled through the canyon walls, sending small whitecaps across the water. Then, out of nowhere, a sharp knock reverberated against the underside of the kayak, jolting us.

"Whoa!" I yelped, grabbing the sides of the boat.

"What was *that*?"

"I ... I don't know," Greg stammered.

But before we could react, the boat lurched again—this time with enough force to nearly tip us. Shadow barked furiously, her eyes fixed on the water, as if something were swimming just beneath the surface.

I leaned over the edge, staring into the murky depths. "Greg, what if there's something down there?"

Greg's eyes followed my gaze, but all we saw was the dark water swirling unnaturally. Another jolt hit the kayak, this time stronger, sending all of us tumbling sideways and into the lake.

Cold water engulfed us, and chaos ensued. Greg resurfaced first, gasping for air, then quickly he scanned the water for me. I popped up a few feet away, sputtering, with Shadow swimming toward me. Her expression was frantic.

"What the hell was that?" I gasped for breath, searching the surrounding water, and trying to keep my eighty-pound Labrador from drowning me as she clawed for me to hold her.

"I don't know!" Greg called back, paddling and grabbing hold of the overturned kayak. "But we need to get back to shore. Now!"

I managed Shadow as we struggled to flip the kayak upright, our movements sluggish in the cold, choppy water. By the time we finally managed to pull ourselves back into the boat, the wind had died down just as quickly as it had come, leaving a bizarre calm in its wake.

Shivering and breathless, we paddled back toward the dock, neither of us speaking, both too shaken to make sense of what had just happened.

CHAPTER THREE

Later that evening, back at home, Greg sat on the couch, staring blankly at his phone. Every time he thought he'd found an impeccable occasion to propose, something inexplicable happened. First, the hike, now the lake. It was as if the universe were conspiring against him. Thank goodness he'd forgotten the ring in the truck when they went out on the lake. Had the day gone well, that would have worked against him, but as it was, he preferred that outcome over the diamond resting somewhere at the bottom of the lake. That reminded him he still needed to retrieve it from the truck and now would be a good time before Libby got out of the shower.

He grabbed his keys and went outside. Shadow followed behind, curious about where they were going.

Opening his truck, he opened the center console, which revealed his locked safe. Moving the dials to the correct code, he punched the button and opened it. He glanced behind him to be sure Libby hadn't come out of the house, then quickly stashed the small box in his pants pocket. Shadow sat, staring patiently, then followed him back into the house.

Hearing that the water was still running, he hurried to the bedroom. Shadow chased behind him, certain a treat would result from this fun game he'd started. Risking a quick look, he carefully opened the box, seeing the two-carat princess cut diamond shining brightly. His heart warmed, more excited than ever to carry through with a romantic proposal.

The water shutting off startled Greg. He quickly stashed the little black box in the nightstand drawer and bolted for the living room, took his spot on the sectional sofa, and encouraged Shadow to join him. She panted happily and accepted the invitation by jumping up and finding her cozy corner.

Now in her warm fuzzy pajamas, Libby curled up next to him on the sofa, flipping through her own phone. "I can't believe the lake today," she said, shaking her head. "Have you ever been on it when it got that rough? I mean, we capsized!"

Greg chuckled half-heartedly. "Yeah, it wasn't exactly what I had in mind. I don't think it was the weather though—I mean, it wasn't *that* windy. There was something in the water. Had to have been." He shuddered, imagining what was so large that it could tip a kayak, and then quickly put it out of his mind.

As they snuggled on the sofa, she read her book,

and he absently scrolled through the information he'd been researching using his phone. Something caught his eye—an article about the Four Peaks Wilderness and the amethyst mine they'd stumbled upon. Lexi was right. With his interest piqued, Greg clicked on it and read.

His eyes widened as he learned the mine was, in fact, still operational—just not in the way they'd expected. It said that in recent years they had reopened it for limited production, but what really grabbed his attention was the mention of special helicopter tours that took visitors directly to the mine.

"Hey hon. Did you know they run tours to the amethyst mine?" Greg asked, catching her attention. "Apparently, it's active, and you can fly to get there. They only offer tours twice a year."

She looked up from her book, raising an eyebrow. "Seriously? It looked totally abandoned to me. At least from what we could see."

"I know," Greg replied absentmindedly, reading through more details. "You know, I suspect what we saw wasn't the actual mine, but I do think we found the property. There's a little map here and I think the actual operations are on the other side of that ridgeline. Maybe where we were was another abandoned mine? Or it could have been some opening, er, mineshaft at another point in the mountain from where they work?" He kept reading and providing more information. "This is incredible, hon. It would be interesting to see the operation officially. Flying in sure would be easier than that hike."

Her eyes lit up. "Oooh, a helicopter ride would be fun."

Greg smiled, the gears turning in his head again. Maybe *this* was how it was supposed to all unfold—the ultimate surprise proposal. A helicopter ride, a mine tour, and finally that undeniable moment to pop the question he'd delayed asking so many times.

"You'd go back there again?" he asked, his excitement building, but still surprised they'd consider it after their experience.

She shrugged, looking slightly wary. "I mean, if it was an organized thing, sure," she agreed. "With a group of other people and a guide? Yes. And as long as we don't go back to that place where I fell into the earth. Sure, I'd be up for it."

"Yeah," he said, having lost all previous concerns. "I think we should go. Could be an unforgettable adventure." He winked, giving her arm a loving squeeze as he took down the details to give the company a call.

* * *

The next day at work, I told Lexi how our outdoor adventure had gone haywire again. She was in disbelief, but was also excited to hear what Greg learned about those mine tours.

"If there's room, I think that's something JJ would like to do as well. I mean, I'm not inviting ourselves on your romantic getaway…"

"Oh, don't be silly. Romantic getaway." I scoffed. "We'd love to do it as a group. I'll let you know what we find out."

"We could also go out to Canyon Lake anytime as a group, too. You know we have the boat—much sturdier than going out in a kayak." She looked up from her computer. "I would love to know what was so large that could tip that kayak over, though. That's a crazy story."

I shivered, thinking about how terrifying it was in the water. Was there something down there that tipped us? Or was it a rogue wave the wind conjured up? Shadow pawed at my leg, bringing my attention back to the conversation with Lexi, but it also had me wondering whether my dog had just read my mind.

My phone chimed. I held up my index finger for Lexi to hold on a second and I pulled it from my pocket.

"Hi, Mom. How's the Christmas bazaar at the church going?"

"Oh honey, so many people showed up. The ladies and I have nearly sold all our knitting!"

"That's fantastic. And you're still set to move back to your home this week?"

"Yes, that's right. I'm sure Margie is counting the minutes until I move out." She chuckled, and then I heard Margie protesting in the background. "I was calling to see if you and Greg were still planning on spending the holiday at his place in the mountains?"

"Yep, we're headed to Heber as soon as I get off work tomorrow afternoon." I heard her huge sigh. "Did you need something before we go?"

"No. I was hoping you'd changed your mind and would spend Christmas with us."

"At Margie's?"

"Of course."

"Well, I didn't know she was planning something. You never mentioned that before. But we've already decided to get away this holiday. The last one wore me out."

"I understand, honey." Her words were sweet, but I heard the disappointment and it brought immediate guilt.

"Will Jordan be joining you?"

"I doubt it. She's still pretty upset with me."

"Oh dear," I said under my breath, remembering the letter we'd found while cleaning out my mother's home after her kitchen caught fire before Thanksgiving. "I'd thought she'd come around by now."

"Would you talk to her, Libby? You're always so good with your sister."

My brows furrowed in disbelief. My sister and I seldom fully agreed on things, and I felt like she never paid attention to what I had to say. However, I was curious about her point of view on the news about our father.

"I have to stop by her house later today. I'll see what I can do. No promises though, Mom. You probably should give her more time—she'll come around. If nothing else, I'm sure she'll need a sitter soon enough."

"Hm. Well, let me know what she has to say. I just don't know what to do."

Lexi overheard portions of the conversation, and when I hung up, curiosity got the best of her. "Jordan isn't speaking to Julia? Why?"

After everything that had gone wrong over Thanksgiving, I kind of mentally shuttered myself away for a few weeks. Had I really not yet confided in my best friend about the revelations related to my father's death, years ago?

I glanced at my watch, grimacing. "Hey, I have a massage appointment starting in about ten minutes. I have so much to fill you in on. How about happy hour, just you and me, after work?"

"Deal. Let's say at five?"

"Sure. That will give me time to go by my sister's house first. I'll meet you at the sushi place at five."

After I'd completed the massage session with my client, I drove over to Jordan's house. My niece, Apple, opened the door, giving me a big hug and then running off to her room. It seemed more and more these days that's where the teens—Apple and Annie—hung out. The younger ones—Ryan and Chase—were in a fierce battle of Mario Kart in their playroom.

"Would you like a cup of tea?" my sister asked.

I nodded and took a seat at the kitchen counter.

"What are your plans for Christmas?" I asked. "Are you splitting the day with Pat again this year?" I knew it was always a juggle for her with the co-parenting around the holidays.

"He's actually away with his new girlfriend's family, so I get the kids all to myself this week. Next week, they'll go over to his house."

"You know, Mom really wants to see you and the kids."

Jordan hung her head. "I know."

"What is it? Why still so upset?"

"She lied to us, Libby."

"I don't think it was on purpose. And I'm not sure she had a choice."

"Maybe not when we were teens, and when Dad passed away. But certainly, plenty of years have passed since we've become adults. She could have come forward with the information before now. For goodness sake, Libby, we're both nearly forty! Well, me closer than you … but you know."

Nodding, I completely agreed with her that our mother should have divulged the big secret. "So, what do you need from her now? You can't just completely turn your back on her."

"Oh, yeah?" Her eyebrow lifted. "What else is she lying about?" She poured tea into two mugs and handed me one.

"Oh, c'mon, Jordan. She literally was trying to protect us. I think you, as a mom yourself, could understand that. Despite what we think now, her intentions were good *at the time*."

"Well, then why didn't she stand up for Dad more? Why didn't she move heaven and earth to find out answers about the people who killed him?"

I took a sip of tea, giving myself a second to think about her question. I'd had similar thoughts over the past few weeks since learning that his insurance adjuster job may hold the secrets to his death. A heart attack, we'd been told all along. How was it possible to fake a heart attack?

"She told me she went to the police," I simply stated.

"Yeah, and it ended there. She did *nothing* to prompt them to further investigate."

"Do we know that for a fact?" I mumbled, swirling my tea around in the mug.

She shook her head. "I guess not. But she admitted no one has ever gone to jail for his murder."

I looked up at her. "Jordan, it wasn't *murder*."

"How do you know?"

"Because the coroners labeled it as coronary arrest."

"Yeah, but even Mom said there was more to it. She indicated to us *someone* was responsible. Isn't that murder?"

I sighed. "Oh, I'm not sure. But I think we need more information before declaring something as strong as *murder*, don't you?"

"I suppose." She sipped her tea and asked if I wanted a snack.

"No, I'm meeting Lexi after this for sushi."

Her facial expression showed that food group wasn't high on her list.

"Hey, you've done this kind of thing before, Libby. Why aren't you looking into this?"

"What?" I nearly snorted my tea.

"Researched ... you know, investigated people's deaths. Why aren't you jumping right on this? Why not look into our father's death? Mom sure didn't."

"Oh, jeez, Jordan. Can't we just accept that he passed away from a heart attack?" I asked, not admitting to her I'd already had similar thoughts. And really, I'd been trying to convince myself to drop that train of thought and instead focus on my work and my relationship with Greg.

"Please..." she begged me.

"Will you give Mom a break, then?"

Gradually, her smile emerged. "I'll take the kids over to see her on Christmas."

That was good enough for me. "Alright. I can't make any promises about what the outcome will be, but I will promise to look into the circumstances surrounding Dad's death. *If* there's anything to it, I'll follow through until the culprits are in jail."

She came around the counter and gave me an enormous hug. "Let me know how I can help."

Before meeting Lexi at the sushi bar, I dropped my car off at home, fed Shadow and let her out, and then walked over to the restaurant. The crisp evening air was exactly what I needed. My mind swirled with ideas about how to get started investigating my father's death. Even though Jordan seemed confident it was something I did regularly, that was far from the truth.

I thought I could start by accessing public records to obtain the autopsy report, and then maybe inquire with the police about any other related reports. I tried to remember the name of the insurance company my father worked for. As a teen, I held little interest in what he did for a living and it wouldn't have mattered, anyway. I'd never actually understood any of it then. Hopefully, my mother would fill in those gaps for me. And I also hoped that the insurance company still existed—it'd been twenty-three years since his death.

Walking through the parking lot, I saw Lexi had beaten me there. I opened the door to a large jovial gathering, and I found her chatting it up with a couple of people at the bar. As soon as I walked up, she handed me a glass of wine.

"Libby, this is Rob and Tony. I was just telling them all about our business here in Mesa. They showed interest and said their wives would love a spa day." She winked.

I greeted them and shook their hands. "And where do you work?"

Tony was quick to answer. "I'm a historian, currently teaching over at the Central Arizona community college, actually. Rob is an investment broker. Both kind of boring compared to what you two do for a living."

We laughed and exchanged business cards.

I pulled up our latest promotion on my phone and showed the gentlemen. "Seriously, if you're looking for gifts for your wives, we have holiday gift cards on sale right now. Here's the QR code."

They both held their phones up and captured the promotion.

Rob held his hand out again. "Thank you, ladies. We've

gotta get going, but we'll definitely be seeing you again soon."

"Drumming up business wherever we go, huh?" I teased Lexi as we watched them leave the restaurant.

"Don't you know it..." she laughed, then asked, "Should we get a table for more privacy, or are you good here at the bar?"

I looked around, seeing there were some tables still available, so I opted for that.

"So, what's all this family drama?" my friend inquired.

I explained how I'd found the mysterious box while helping my mom clear her house of salvageable items after the fire. Within that box, there was a letter to her from my late father. It was very simple and basically only said he was sorry. Well, that and he also mentioned something to the effect of if she was reading the letter, it meant 'they found' him.

"Who're *they*?" she asked.

I shrugged. "Great question. We don't know. My mom only knew that one case he worked on turned up something that scared him. A lot."

"Case?"

"Oh, he was an insurance adjuster. I honestly don't even know all the ins and outs. But apparently, I'm going to learn!"

"Uh-oh. What does that mean?"

"Jordan practically begged me to look into his death."

"You really think it was something more than a heart attack?"

"I don't know what to think, honestly." I took another sip of wine. "All this has brought up so many feelings again—everything from anger, sadness, denial, and now simply disbelief. Anyway, after getting away in nature with Greg recently, I was ready to bury it and pretend I never learned this new information."

"But it's not that easy, is it?"

"No, not at all. And now Jordan's being insistent about it, too."

"So, what are you going to do?"

"Well, I'm going to do a little digging and we'll see where it goes. Honestly, I hope it goes nowhere."

The server came around and we ordered our favorite sushi rolls and some hot and sour soup. When he asked if we'd like another glass of wine, I was all in. Lexi hesitated.

"I walked, so I'm good. I'm sure one of the guys would walk over and drive your car home." It was nice to live so close to our favorite sushi place.

She agreed and ordered another glass, then picked up her phone to contact JJ.

"So, you and Greg are going up north for the holiday?"

"Yep, and I hear they got some snow already. I'm excited to sit by a fire and relax for a couple of days. It's really been nonstop since Thanksgiving."

"I'd say it's been nonstop for you since before that Alaska trip."

I held up my glass up in agreement. "True! Cheers to us…" Our glasses clinked.

"You need a break from family, Libby. From everything."

"Oh! Greg texted earlier that he'd call about the mine tour. I'll let you know what he learns. I'm not sure when it would be—but I let him know you were interested, too."

"He didn't mind?"

"Of course not! He loves doing stuff with you guys. In fact, it's felt as though we haven't done anything in so long."

"Other than the occasional dinner, you're right. We haven't gone off on a big adventure since we got back from the big RV trip to Utah last year. We'll have to plan another long trip somewhere—until then, we'll continue living vicariously through you both. You two seem to always be exploring something."

Over the course of the evening, we chatted more about family holiday stuff and then caught up on some business talk, too. After ordering and consuming two more rolls, we called it a night. JJ strolled in, looking for his wife just as I finished paying

"Want a ride, Libby?" he offered.

"Thank you. But, no, I think I could use the exercise. It's such a beautiful night."

We all said our goodbyes, promising to get together after Christmas when we returned from the mountains.

CHAPTER FOUR

The idea of proposing during a helicopter tour over the amethyst mine filled Greg with new hope. That was it. After the failed attempts during their hiking trip and the bizarre event at Canyon Lake, the helicopter tour seemed like a foolproof blend of adventure and romance. Plus, it offered a way to embrace the mysteriousness of the mine without risking another unsettling encounter.

He immediately reached out to the company offering the tours and booked the seats for one week away—New Year's Eve. Everything felt like it was finally falling into place.

Until Libby came home and announced that Lexi and JJ were interested in going.

"Oh no. I've already booked it," Greg told her.

Looking dejected, she simply said, "I'm not sure how

to tell Lexi. Could we rebook for another time?"

He pulled her in close. "Let me see what I can do. If it's not possible to change it, let's do it on our own this time. If it's cool, we'll take them again when the mine opens up for tours again."

He wasn't sure if she was completely satisfied with that, but he felt relieved when she shifted the conversation to discuss the visit with her sister. As he listened, he couldn't keep his mind from drifting back to his upcoming plans. Not only the helicopter trip to the mine, but there was still packing to do before their Christmas trip. He could picture the two of them in front of the fireplace, with snow falling outside, sipping hot drinks. Feeling conflicted, maybe that would have been a better moment for his proposal? Nah. New Year's Eve on the top of Four Peaks would sure be the ideal story to tell.

"I think Jordan is more fixed on this being a crime than I am, don't you think?"

He snapped his attention back into the conversation and nodded his head. "Oh, I thought you were concerned and leaned that direction as well, though."

"Yeah. I keep going back and forth. I guess that's why I decided to look into the circumstances."

"What? What exactly do you mean 'look into', Libby? I'm not sure you really need to get involved."

She stopped, turning toward Greg. "That's what I just finished telling you all about!"

"Right. Yes, of course." He leaned in for a kiss. "I'm concerned it could get risky, though. After getting away from those thugs at Thanksgiving, I thought we agreed we'd focus on active and fun stuff for the two of us to do. We agreed to stop getting involved in these dangerous situations."

She scooted closer. "Who says it'll be dangerous? I mean, it's my dad and I have to know what actually happened. Plus, I promised Mom to help mediate between her and Jordan. And because of that, I promised Jordan I'd research our father's death."

"Your Mom needs help to talk with her own daughter?"

"It's like you heard nothing I told you."

He blushed. "I promise I'll do better. There's been a lot to consider recently. And I'm a little distracted with Christmas plans and the upcoming helicopter trip. Excited, you know?"

She snuggled up to him. "So am I."

* * *

After the two-hour drive the next day, Libby breathed in the crisp afternoon mountain air, her cheeks tingling as a gust of icy wind brushed past. Snowflakes clung to her wool hat, melting against her skin as she stood on the porch of Greg's cabin. The log cabin, tucked away in the snowy pines of Heber, was one of her favorite places— cozy, secluded, and sublime for a quiet Christmas escape. Shadow sniffed around the porch, content.

"Beautiful, huh?" Greg said, coming up and wrapping his arms around her waist. His breath was warm against her ear.

"I've never been here in winter," she said, leaning back into him. "It's so quiet. Peaceful."

"That's the best part," Greg replied. "No city noise, no distractions. Just us." He kissed the top of her head. "You ready for the first adventure, though?"

Libby turned, grinning. "Snowshoeing, right? I've never done it."

"Don't worry, I'll show you the ropes." Greg nodded toward a pair of snowshoes leaning against the cabin. "We'll head out into the forest. There's a great trail that leads to a lookout point. Perfect day hike."

Libby couldn't help but feel a surge of excitement. She and Greg had been through so much lately with the mystery of her father's death looming over her But here, in the quiet of the snow-covered woods, it felt like they could finally be alone. No distractions, no investigations—just them.

Bundling up in thick jackets, scarves, and gloves, they strapped on their snowshoes and the cute booties onto Shadow's feet and set off into the woods. At first, the snowshoeing was awkward—Libby's legs felt like they were learning to walk all over again—but soon she fell into a rhythm and got the hang of it. Greg led the way, their snowshoes crunching through the powder as they trekked deeper into the forest. Shadow ran ahead of them, then bolted back, frolicking in the snow.

The trees were tall and dusted with snow, their branches hanging heavy with icicles. It was like stepping into a winter wonderland. Every now and then, Greg would stop and point out something—animal tracks in the snow, a hawk soaring overhead, or the way the sunlight broke through the branches, casting a golden glow on the white winter landscape.

After a while, they reached a clearing at the top of a small hill. Greg helped her up onto a rocky outcrop, and when she stood up, her breath caught in her throat. The view was breathtaking. Below them, the forest stretched out for miles, a sea of white and green. Beyond that, the snow-capped Mogollon Rim loomed in the distance.

"Merry Christmas," Greg said, his voice soft.

Libby turned to him, smiling. "It's breathtaking."

They stood there for a long pause, hand in hand, watching the sun dip lower in the sky. The peace and beauty of the wilderness felt like a gift all its own, one that they both desperately needed. He regretted only for a second not bringing the ring along; however, he had resigned himself to believing that the helicopter trip to the Four Peaks Wilderness would be the prime opportunity. He was sure she hadn't suspected a thing, despite his efforts to keep her mother quiet for months now.

Shadow led their way back to the cabin, as the sky darkened, and the first twinkling stars appeared overhead. Greg built a fire in the hearth, and the cabin glowed warmly, welcoming them back. Inside, they peeled off their snowy clothes, hanging them by the fire to dry.

Later that night, after a simple dinner and a glass of wine, Libby curled up on the couch, wrapped in a blanket. He sat beside her, his arm around her shoulders, the flicker of the fire reflecting in his eyes.

"This is exactly what I needed," she whispered, resting her head against him. "Just us."

He smiled, kissing her temple. "It's not over yet. Tomorrow, we're meeting up with some friends—don't worry, it's low key. Just a few folks from the area and some of my forest service buddies. We'll hike, maybe sled a little. Trust me, you'll love them."

Libby sighed contentedly. "As long as I'm with you, I'm up for anything."

CHAPTER FIVE

The next morning, I woke to the smell of coffee and the sound of bacon sizzling on the stove. Stretching and smiling to myself as the cabin's warmth enveloped me, I quickly pulled out my laptop and fired it up. Before heading downstairs, I wanted to do a couple of quick internet searches. I had woken up wondering about the insurance case my dad was working on at the time of his death, and I couldn't let it go.

Typing in my browser, I searched for insurance companies, hoping that one would trigger a memory for me. After scrolling through pages of information, I realized this was a ridiculous way to proceed. I picked up my phone off the nightstand and texted my mother.

What insurance company did Dad work for?

A few seconds later…

Frontier Fidelity. Why? Surely you're not doing this on Christmas Day!

Love you, Mom. Merry Christmas!

I spent several more minutes searching the company and making some notes about the current leadership, then googling news articles related to my father, Leon Madsen. There were none, but his obituary popped up, which created a swell in my heart as soon as I saw the familiar photograph. I shut the lid on my laptop, closing my eyes, and wondering again what I was doing dredging up these past hurts.

When I padded into the kitchen, Greg was already dressed in a flannel shirt, flipping pancakes like a pro.

"Breakfast is served," he said, grinning at me as I entered.

"You're spoiling me," I teased, moving in behind him and carefully giving him a squeeze around his middle. "Merry Christmas!"

"Only the best for you," Greg replied, pouring coffee into a mug and ushering me to the table. "Eat up. We've got plans today." Before I took a seat, he leaned over for a kiss. "And Merry Christmas to you, too, my love."

After breakfast, we geared up in our warm layers once again and headed into town, where we met up with Greg's friends at a local café. The group was made up of some of Greg's fellow forest rangers and a couple of old friends from the area—people who had grown up exploring the woods and mountains of Heber.

They instantly welcomed me, joking and laughing easily; camaraderie that made me feel at home even among strangers.

"Ready for a real adventure?" Greg's friend Brian asked, slinging a pack over his shoulder.

"What do you have in mind?" I asked, curious.

"We're heading to one of our favorite spots," Greg explained. "A little-known sledding hill just outside of town. It's tucked away, so no tourists—just us."

The drive out to the hill was scenic, with snow-covered trees lining the road and the occasional deer crossing our path. Shadow gave a cheerful sounding bark when she saw them. When we arrived, the group unloaded sleds and we made our way up the hill, laughing like kids as we trudged through the snow.

I couldn't help but giggle too; the joy was infectious as we reached the top and took turns racing down the hill. The thrill of the sledding, the chilly wind whipping through my hair, reminded me of childhood winters, but it felt even better now, with Shadow chasing me, and Greg cheering me on from the bottom of the hill.

After hours of sledding and a quick stop for hot cocoa, we invited the group back to Greg's cabin. There, we gathered around a fire pit in the yard, roasting marshmallows and swapping stories. Greg's ranger friends shared tales of close encounters with wildlife, while I told funny stories from my time with Greg as well.

As the fire crackled, Greg leaned in close to me, his arm around my shoulders. "Having fun?" he asked.

I smiled up at him. "The best." Shadow kept my feet warm as she snoozed near the fire, exhausted from the full day's adventures.

The night ended with everyone saying their goodbyes and Greg and I retreating inside the cabin. As we sat by the fire inside the house, sipping a glass of wine, I couldn't help but feel overwhelmed with happiness. The simple pleasures—the snow, the company, the warmth of Greg beside me—made this Christmas one I'd never forget.

And as we sat in comfortable silence, watching the flames dance in the fireplace, I knew that this—this quiet, peaceful moment—was exactly what we both needed.

As the sun rose the next morning and the last embers of the fire had long since cooled, the cabin felt a little too quiet as I pulled my sweater tighter around me. The twinkling Christmas lights Greg had strung up along the cabin's rafters earlier were still glowing softly, casting a warm golden hue over the living room. But it was time to take them down, pack up, and head back to reality.

I sighed, glancing out the frosted window. The snow-covered woods outside had been our sanctuary for the past couple of days, and the thought of leaving this peaceful place left a knot in my chest.

Greg appeared from the bedroom, pulling on his coat. "You all set?" he asked, his voice gentle.

I smiled wistfully. "I just hate that it's already over."

Greg nodded, crossing the room and wrapping his arms around me from behind. He rested his chin on my shoulder. "I know. I wish we could stay here forever."

Leaning into him and closing my eyes, I savored the last quiet alone-time in the cabin. "It's been so lovely."

Greg kissed the top of my head. "We'll be back soon. This place is always here for us when we need it."

We lingered a little longer, both reluctant to break the spell of the holiday, but eventually, the sound of the wind outside reminded us that the world was waiting. Greg squeezed my hand. "Come on. Let's get everything packed up."

As we loaded the car, the snow fell again, light flurries swirling around. I watched the cabin disappear from view in the rearview mirror as we drove down the winding road, feeling a pang of sadness. The magic of our secluded Christmas had come to an end.

The drive back to Phoenix was mostly quiet, but not an uncomfortable one. It was the kind of quiet shared between two people who had found peace, who didn't need to fill every second with conversation.

About halfway through the trip, Greg cleared his throat. "You okay?"

I nodded, glancing over at him. "Yeah, I'm fine. Just … thinking about everything we're going back to."

Greg's jaw tightened slightly, but he didn't let it linger. "We'll figure it out. Whatever comes next."

I smiled at him, grateful for his devotion. "I know."

When we pulled into the driveway around noon, the few festive decorations I had put up after Thanksgiving looked oddly out of place. The blinking lights and wreath on the door seemed to mock the end of the holiday, as if daring me to hold on to the cheer for just a little longer. Well, I would—I wasn't giving in to the end of everything merry yet.

Greg helped me bring in the bags, and as we stood inside the entryway, I turned to him. "Promise we'll do that more—get away to the mountains?"

Greg smiled, brushing a strand of hair from my face. "Promise."

The warmth of his smile made it easier to transition back to normal life, and soon we settled on the couch, surrounded by unpacked bags but not in any rush to deal with them. I curled up against Greg, feeling the familiar comfort of being home but still carrying the peace of the cabin with me.

We spent the rest of the afternoon in quiet companionship, making plans for the coming week. Greg had a few shifts at work, and I had my share of massage appointments to tend to. Most importantly, I wanted to dive into the investigation into my father's death. We also both looked forward to our New Year's Eve adventure the following weekend, and I still held out hope that Greg could get Lexi and JJ added to the passenger list. Whatever loomed ahead, we allowed ourselves one last evening of calm.

Later, as the lights dimmed and Greg's breathing became soft and even beside me, I lay awake, staring at the ceiling. I knew our Christmas escape had been a brief respite, and now we were about to step back into the storm. But something about the time we'd shared made me feel stronger—more ready to face whatever came next.

And as I finally drifted off to sleep, my hand resting in Greg's, I knew that no matter what challenges lay ahead, he was right by my side.

CHAPTER SIX

I sat on the floor of my living room, boxes scattered around. My father's old work files, tucked away in a storage unit for years, now lay open. Oddly, I felt nostalgic running my fingers over the faded labels. They were all neatly organized—just as my father had always been. He was meticulous, both in life and in work.

How could someone so organized, so careful, die so young from a heart attack? The official cause of death had never made sense for someone so young, so vital. But I never questioned it. Not until now.

My phone buzzed on the coffee table. JJ's name flashed across the screen. I hesitated, then answered.

"You find anything yet?" JJ's voice was low, cautious.

"I've been rifling through the boxes for hours now,"

I answered, grateful that he'd agreed to guide me along. "There are so many files here, JJ. It's daunting."

"Start with anything that stands out. Any big cases he was working on in the weeks and months before he died."

When he said that, I went back to one file I'd seen earlier. A file marked **Coronado Estate Fire**. I hadn't recognized the estate name, but noticed the date was a week before my father's death. "There's a case here about a fire at some estate. I don't remember him ever talking about this."

"Coronado Estate," JJ repeated. "That rings a bell. Hold on."

I heard his keyboard clicking as he quieted. "Yeah, that was a big fire—total loss. The owner was a local real estate developer, Thomas Coronado. That guy had his hands in a lot of shady deals. Are you saying your dad worked that case?"

My heartbeat quickened. "It looks like it. Why?"

"Coronado has connections," JJ said, his voice dropping. "Big connections. Some of the stuff he's involved in, it's been hard to pin anything on him, but there's always a whisper about organized crime, money laundering, arson for insurance payouts. If your dad was looking into one of his properties, that could've put him on a dangerous path."

I stared at the file in my hands. The pieces didn't fit. "My dad was an insurance adjuster, JJ. He dealt with paperwork. How would that get him killed?"

"Maybe he found something he wasn't supposed to," JJ suggested. "Look, I'll check what I can from my end. But if your dad was sniffing around Coronado, we need to be careful."

My stomach knotted. "What do you mean?"

"I mean, I've heard a lot of things about that guy and his organization. Coronado could have some high-level people in his back pocket, too—I just don't know. If your dad found something, they might've been the ones to cover it up. I'll dig quietly, but I need to keep this off the books. No official investigation. Not yet."

Nodding, even though he couldn't see me, I closed the file and leaned back against the wall feeling the enormity of the secrets my father had left behind. "I don't know what to think, JJ. This doesn't feel real."

"It's real, Libby. And if you want to find out what really happened to your dad, we're going to have to play it smart. Look for anything unusual in his files—anything that might've caught his attention before he died. I'll run background checks on the people involved in the fire and see what I can find on Coronado. But we're walking on eggshells here. One wrong move, and they'll know we're looking."

I swallowed down the lump in my throat. "Alright. And no, I'm not backing down."

"I didn't think you would," JJ said, a hint of a smile in his voice. "I'll be in touch. Stay safe, Libs."

As the call ended, I looked back down at the file in my lap. **Coronado Estate Fire**. The papers inside detailed the damage, the claims made by Coronado, and the cause of the fire—a supposed electrical failure.

But as I flipped through the pages, something caught my eye. A handwritten note in my father's neat script. *Possible arson? Check accelerants.*

My breath hitched, realizing my father had suspected something wasn't right. And if he'd followed that trail, it might have led him to something—or someone—

dangerous enough to silence him.

I set the file aside and reached for another, heart racing, and knowing this was just the beginning.

* * *

My thoughts whirled the rest of the morning as I tried to do my day job. Thankfully, my client was a quiet one, and not the type who chattered nonstop. As I went through the motions of Ashiatsu therapy, I kept thinking back to the Coronado case. Clearly, my father suspected arson. That alone could have put him in danger if what JJ was saying about this man was true.

Then I remembered the laptop I'd found along with the loads of file boxes. I prayed it would fully charge while I was away all day at work. The next challenge would be breaking its passcode to get in. If I could get into my dad's email, or any other notes he may have kept on his computer, it would be so helpful. So far, it appeared he liked to scribe his notes, but I was eager to find out what was on that computer.

After finishing three massage sessions, I quickly cleaned the rooms and rushed into the office to get my purse and my dog. Shadow lifted her head from the bed she was napping in as I entered, not in any hurry to be roused.

Lexi greeted me with her smile. "You're in a hurry."

I hadn't seen her since we'd gotten home from the mountains. Even as eager as I was to get back to those boxes and that computer, it wouldn't hurt to slow down and spend some time with my business partner. Shadow sat on my feet while I stroked her fur.

Lexi told me about her son, Joshua, being over the moon about getting a new bike, a 'big boy' bike, for Christmas. JJ hadn't mentioned that when I was on the phone with him earlier. He'd been all business.

"Is that a Christmas present, too?" I pointed out the diamond that hung delicately at the nape of her neck.

"Oh! Yes! Look what JJ splurged on." She leaned over the desk and I got a closer look.

"It's gorgeous."

"What did you get?" she asked, making no secret of staring at my left hand.

"You know, we didn't exchange gifts. Which we agreed about ahead of time—don't worry! But we had such a magical time up in the mountains. It's hard to describe, but everything was simple and flawless."

Her smile illuminated. "You two are so darned cute." She shuffled a few papers around the desk and then looked up at me and asked, "So, why in such a hurry today?"

"Oh, I've found some things related to my dad's last investigation. I guess I'm excited to get back to it."

She nodded, locking her desk drawer, and looking back at me. "And what did Greg find out about the mine tour? Are we going?"

I'd completely forgotten, but Greg had informed me earlier that they were unable to add anyone else on the flight. "Well, um … yes and no. Apparently, he got the last two seats on the helicopter…"

Lexi's smile fell. "Oh, dang. I was really hoping…"

"I know! He said it's super difficult to get a reservation, and I hadn't told him yet that you two were interested. So, we figured we'll go and if it's really something, then we'll try again another time for the four of us?"

She nodded, deflated. "Yeah. Let us know."

I stood and rounded her desk. "I'm so sorry. I wish it would have worked out."

"When are you going?" she asked.

"New Year's Eve."

Her eyes widened with surprise. "Oh, that's soon."

* * *

The sun was setting by the time Shadow and I made it back home. Greg was away for work and would return the next day, which meant that I had all evening to rummage through the boxes still sitting on my living room floor.

First, I took Shadow outside and threw the ball for her. We hadn't gone on our run that morning, but I was eager to get back to that paperwork. Back inside, I dished up her food and heard my phone buzz—JJ.

"Libby, I found something," he said, without even a hello. His voice was urgent. "I ran a background check on Thomas Coronado. Nothing unusual on the surface, but I dug deeper into his connections. His name came up in connection with a series of other fires—properties he owned, businesses he invested in. But there's a pattern. Every time, the payout was massive. Every time, they listed the cause of the fire as accidental."

"You're saying these fires weren't accidents?"

"I'm saying Coronado has been using fires to cash in on insurance money for years," JJ said. "And your dad might've been the only one smart enough to catch onto it. That note you found? About the accelerants? Your dad was looking into arson. I think he knew Coronado was behind it."

I sank into a chair, overwhelmed. My father may have uncovered a massive insurance fraud scheme, and it had gotten him killed. "What do we do now?"

"There's more," JJ said, his tone dropping lower. "I checked the file on your dad's death. Something's off. The medical examiner who ruled it a heart attack? He's had other cases come under scrutiny—cases where the cause of death didn't match up with the evidence. He's covered up suspicious deaths before, probably on Coronado's orders."

I felt my blood run cold. "So, my dad didn't die of a heart attack?"

"I'm not sure we can say that for certain," JJ said. "But there are ways to induce a heart attack that don't leave obvious traces—drugs, for one. The thing is, without reopening the case officially, we can't just go in and demand another autopsy. We need solid proof your dad was murdered, and that will not be easy."

I clenched my fists. "There has to be something in his files, something he was working on before he died. If I can find out what he knew—"

"Slow down," JJ interrupted. "We're talking about a powerful guy with a lot of dangerous connections. If you start digging too hard, you'll put a target on your back. Coronado's people are everywhere, and you have no idea how far their reach goes. We need to be careful."

"I'm not going to stop, JJ," I said firmly. "He killed my dad. I can't let this go."

"I know how you must feel," JJ sighed. "But we need a plan. I can start working on getting a second look at the medical examiner, maybe get an anonymous tip sent to the state. In the meantime, go through the rest of your dad's files, see if there's anything else he was working on. Look for names, addresses, anything that could connect the dots."

I nodded. "Okay. I'll start tonight."

As we hung up, I stared at the laptop I'd charged. Then I stared at the boxes again. It seemed like a mountain of paper, each file a possible clue, another piece of the puzzle that my father had left behind.

I opened the laptop and tried a password: **jordanlibbyjulia**. It immediately connected, and I chuckled. My father would never fare well in today's cybersecurity world. Opening his file explorer, I scrolled through the folders he had set up. One caught my eye instantly, it was labeled: **Urgent — Coronado Investigation**. My pulse quickened. When I opened it, I found a series of documents that included typed notes, handwritten annotations, and several copies of emails between my father and a man named Nathan Pierce.

I wondered then if my dad's email account would be accessible. When I went back to the home screen, I saw he had Google mail. I clicked on it and after it buffered for several minutes; it opened. Of course, a ton of junk email flowed in. What I was curious about were the communications he received in the months prior to his death, so I typed February 2000 in the search field. When the email listing came up, I sorted by last name. Scrolling down the page, I found Nathan Pierce. There it was, the subject line **Coronado Fire—Critical Info. Call me ASAP.** But the email was marked as unread.

I couldn't believe the search actually worked, but I felt crushed and my breath caught in my throat. This was the last thing my father had been working on before he died, and that weighed heavily on me.

I stared at the name Nathan Pierce, my mind racing. Who was this man, and why hadn't my father opened the email? I quickly typed his name into a search engine, hoping for something—a job, a news article, anything. A hit came up almost immediately.

Nathan Pierce — Private Investigator. Specializing in Arson and Fraud.

My fingers hovered over the keyboard. Had my father been working with a PI? My mom hadn't mentioned that before? I copied down the number listed on Nathan Pierce's website and dialed, taking the chance that he'd be working late.

It rang twice before a gruff voice answered. "Pierce."

I swallowed. "Hi, Mr. Pierce. My name is Libby—Libby Madsen. I think you were in contact with my father before he … before he passed away."

There was a pause on the other end of the line, then a soft curse. "Libby Madsen? You're Leon's kid?"

"Yes," I said, my voice faltering. "I found your name in his files. I think you were working with him on the Coronado fire case."

Pierce let out a long breath. "Yeah, I was. Your dad was onto something big. I didn't realize he—" He stopped himself. "Look, we should talk, but this isn't something I can discuss over the phone."

I felt pounding in my chest. "Okay. When can we meet?"

"Tomorrow. I'll text you an address. And kid … be careful. If someone killed your dad over this, you could be next."

The line went dead.

I lowered the phone, my hands shaking. Tomorrow, I would meet Nathan Pierce, and maybe—just maybe—I'd find out what my father had died for.

But JJ was right. The deeper I dug, the more dangerous it seemed. I just hoped I wasn't too late to uncover the truth.

CHAPTER SEVEN

By the time Greg got back home from his forestry work, he only wanted a cup of coffee and to put his feet up. He sat on the couch, nursing his coffee, staring at the faint glow of the Christmas lights still strung around the living room. They hadn't yet taken them down, despite his teasing her about it being "time to move on." For Libby, those lights weren't just about the holidays—they were about their time in Heber, those few days of quiet, snow, and laughter. Intimate time alone and also the fun escapades with friends.

He took another sip; the warmth contrasted with the chilly night he'd spent working outdoors, and letting his mind drift back to their Christmas getaway. He could still see Libby's face, flushed from the cold as they trudged through the snow in their snowshoes, her laughter ringing out when he'd tried to make a snow angel and ended up with snow down his collar instead. The way she'd clung to him for balance on the icy path, her eyes bright with happiness. There were a thousand brief memories that told him they were ready to make a life together forever.

Greg chuckled to himself, feeling a familiar flutter of nerves. Part of him wondered if he'd already missed that moment, right there with the snow and the glow of the fire behind them. They'd been cozied up in the cabin, and it had been as close to a fairytale as he'd ever felt. But every time he'd thought about it, he'd hesitated, holding back. He wanted the proposal to be different—something they'd never forget. And he wasn't sure the quiet cabin retreat, as beautiful as it was, held quite the adventurous magic he'd imagined for their engagement.

His gaze fell to the magazine on the table, open to an article about the amethyst mine. The photos of brilliant purple crystals glinting in the rocky depths brought him back to his current plan. The tour, the place where their whole mystery-filled journey would begin—*that* felt like the right timing, the right stage. Their earlier trip into the wilderness, and all the setbacks since, had somehow only drawn them closer. He chuckled to himself—with each misstep, the proposal had taken on a life of its own.

He could practically picture it: the helicopter ride, the adrenaline and excitement of being back in that wild, beautiful place, the sense of adventure that had marked their relationship from the start. It would be the ideal proposal—different, meaningful, and unforgettable.

Setting down his mug, he leaned back and crossed his arms across his body. A quiet confidence settled over him.

No, he didn't regret holding back at Christmas. Their time at the cabin would always be special, a beautiful memory in its own right. But for a proposal? He wanted to symbolize how they'd met and everything they'd experienced together so far. That had to happen on their terms, part of their own adventure, similar to how it all began.

Greg smiled, feeling a spark of anticipation as he imagined it in vivid detail. He was sure now. The upcoming mine tour was exactly the right choice. And when he saw the look on Libby's face, he knew he wouldn't question it for a second.

He heard the shower in the other room turn off and it snapped him back into the present. Soon after, she strolled out into the living room, in her fluffy pink robe and her wet auburn hair tied up in a terry cloth turbine.

"You're home!" she exclaimed when she saw him. She rushed over and plopped down beside him. "How was it?"

After he leaned over and planted a kiss on her lips, he simply stated, "Cold."

She giggled. "Well, I'm glad you found some hot coffee, then." She tilted her head toward his steaming mug sitting on the bedside table. She stood and apologized for her mess all over their living room floor.

"You're deep into it now, aren't you?"

She grinned. "Don't worry. I'll get it picked up."

"Have you learned anything new since I've been away?"

"I think so. JJ has been a great help and I'm meeting with the private investigator whom my father had worked with years ago."

Greg's eyebrows lifted. "Wow. So, they think there is really something to this?"

"Could be. Uncertain, though."

She filled him in on the few conversations, and showed him the paperwork related to the Coronado house fire.

"Please be careful, Libby."

"Of course. Want some breakfast?" She scurried into the kitchen and scrounged up some items from the refrigerator to make a hearty breakfast for the forest ranger. "I've got to leave in about an hour. You're not working today, are you?"

"Yep, gotta check in at the office."

"Wow, no time for rest. That doesn't seem right."

Greg smiled and helped get the table set for breakfast.

CHAPTER EIGHT

I arrived at the small office tucked away in a long strip of outdated buildings near downtown Mesa. The narrow staircase leading to his upstairs office creaked as I climbed, adding a fittingly gritty ambiance to my nervous anticipation. I found the suite number I was looking for. The simple brass plate on the door read: **Nathan Pierce, Private Investigator**.

Inside, the office was dim, with only a desk lamp casting a warm glow over the papers strewn across his desk. Stacks of files and thick binders filled the shelves along one wall. Nathan Pierce, late-fifties with a weathered look that came from years of work, looked up as I entered, his dark eyes studying me as if he could already read my intentions.

"You're Libby, right?" he asked, his voice smooth

but slightly raspy. "I wasn't sure you'd actually come." He stood and greeted me with a hug, which caught me off guard. Pulling back, but keeping his rough hands on my shoulders, he sighed. "I see the resemblance. And the fact you're here shows you're like him in more ways than one."

I'd heard that many times throughout my adulthood, but wasn't quite sure what to say now. Instead, I accepted the chair he pulled out for me and got right down to business. "I need answers, and I think you're the only one who can help me."

Nathan nodded, settling back in his chair. "Of course, I knew your father. Worked cases with him back in the day. Good man. He trusted his instincts—and his gut was rarely wrong."

My breath hitched slightly. "I think he uncovered something, and it's ... well, it's haunting me. There are things I've found—names, addresses that he'd marked as 'urgent.'" I held up a small slip of paper where my father had jotted down a handful of details. One name highlighted on the paper was Nathan Pierce.

He took the paper, his face unreadable behind his barely groomed silver facial hair. "I was new in the industry; young and I'd left the police force because of all the bureaucracy. Thought I was smarter than all of them and I ventured out into the private sector to be my own boss. Your father was one of my first clients in the early days of my PI startup." Nathan pushed his chair back from the desk and stood up, slowly making his way to the window. At fifty-five, the man's physique, his upper back slightly hunched forward at the shoulders, and also favoring his right side as he walked, appeared older than his years. Staring out the window, his right hand firm on his hip, he continued. "I helped him with random background checks and finding people, mainly. Also, tracing money."

He turned away from the window and began pacing the length of the linoleum tiled flooring in the room. "Your dad reached out to me just before he passed. Said he'd stumbled onto something big; something dangerous. He wanted my help—but he never got the chance to tell me exactly what it was." Nathan's jaw clenched. "Days later, I heard about his death. I was told he had a heart attack."

Goosebumps lined my arms. "But you don't believe that, do you?"

Nathan's dark brown eyes were piercing. "Well, how that man operated, never letting things go, it didn't truly surprise me." He sat back down at his desk, leaning forward, resting his elbows on the desk. "But it sounded to me as though he might be on to something. I never found out exactly what. Just got a sense he'd dug into something darker than he'd expected."

I sat quietly as I processed his words. "Do you know what cases he'd been handling? Maybe that'd be a clue to his death?"

Nathan nodded. "Oh, as I recall, the usual mix of fraud claims. But one case was different. He was looking into some big claims—arson, theft, multiple high-dollar payouts." His gaze shifted toward the ceiling, deep in thought. "If I'm remembering correctly, he came to me instead of his company's investigators, because they specifically removed him from those cases and were assigning him local claims that were far beneath his years of experience. Come to think of it, I seem to recall he had a distrust in the management there. That's why he reached out to me, hoping I could help him, off the books, so to speak."

"So, you think…" I hesitated. "Someone didn't want

him digging too deep."

"Could be." Nathan's expression softened; his gruff tone was more sincere. "Look, Libby, I wish I'd pushed harder to understand it or that I'd known exactly how urgent it was then. I've always felt a sadness that our last scheduled meeting never happened. But I've kept everything he sent me. If you're serious about this, I'll let you see what I've got. But you have to understand, it's been years now. It's very unlikely you'll find anything. I guess what I'm saying is that you should also prepare yourself. There may be nothing to find. He could have simply died from a heart attack, you know."

I nodded, his words settling over me. "I understand. However, I think there is good reason to look into it." I watched his face as he nodded. With my voice resolute, I added, "I'm ready. And I'd appreciate any help you can give me."

Nathan leaned back in his chair, his face still impassive, but his dark eyes sharper than ever. "If you're serious about getting to the bottom of this, there are some places I can take you. Things I've uncovered myself about your father's case that I never shared with anyone years back."

My curiosity sparked. "Like what?"

Nathan pulled open a drawer and retrieved a slim file, its edges worn. He slid it across the desk. "This is what your father managed to get for me before his death. It's a series of claims he investigated, linked to a few high-profile clients who had a lot to lose. He was connecting dots where no one else could—or maybe just no one else *would*."

I opened the file, my breath catching as I skimmed the first few pages. Names of properties I didn't recognize from the files I had, large insurance claims tied to arson, theft, even a suspicious accident involving an industrial warehouse fire. Each case seemed to share the same thread: large payouts under suspect circumstances, all tied back to high-profile individuals and companies, most of whom had managed to avoid any kind of scrutiny.

"This is…" I spoke softly, glancing up at Nathan. "This is bigger than I thought."

He nodded grimly. "Your father suspected something was going on. He thought these claims were intentional—likely staged to collect big payouts. I'm sure the more he found, the more he saw a pattern of claims that could've sunk Frontier Fidelity. The question is whether any of his findings *prove* it was intentional. He must have believed it was a well-organized, far-reaching scheme."

My pulse quickened. "You think it's what, like a ring?"

Nathan's expression darkened. "Organized insurance fraud, yes. At least, perhaps. I'm not sure there's enough evidence to say for sure. Another reason I never pursued it after he passed away. You have to understand that none of this," his hand swept out over the contents of the file, "nothing he showed me was definitive proof." After letting the implication settle, Nathan continued, "Listen. *If* this was a targeted attack, your father most likely uncovered things that could not only expose a few big clients, but could also bring down the insurance company. People don't take well to exposure."

I was silent, trying to process what Nathan was saying. "Why didn't he just … why didn't he stop?"

Nathan leaned forward; his voice softened. "You know your father. He wasn't the kind to back down from what he thought was right. I'm sure he thought that if he could prove what he'd suspected, he'd be able to put an end to it. But then he realized he was being followed, and that's when he reached out to me." Nathan paused, a hint of regret flashing across his face. "I'm sorry. I didn't understand the urgency of it at the time, or I would've done more."

My fists automatically clenched, my nails digging into my palms. "So, what do we do now?"

"We start where your father left off," Nathan replied. "One of the last places he was seen visiting is an old warehouse on the outskirts of the city," Nathan stated. "It's still abandoned. If we're lucky, we might find some evidence of what he was investigating there."

My eyes flicked back to the file. The warehouse address was marked in red and underlined twice with the word 'urgent.' Just seeing his handwriting, I felt a pang in my chest. "Let's go."

Nathan gave her an approving nod. "Hold on. I've got other work I'm doing, but let me get back to you. And Libby," he added, as we gathered our things, "prepare yourself; this may lead nowhere. Or, we could open Pandora's box. Regardless, let's keep anything we learn closely guarded. If your dad really died because of that investigation, this could be a deadly venture."

His warning left me shaken as I wound my way through the city streets and back to work. What exactly was I doing by opening this up? It didn't matter. I had to follow the leads wherever they took me. Also, JJ would have my back. Nathan seemed like a decent man. My heart sank, remembering my pact with Greg. I know we talked about not getting involved in other people's messes anymore. But certainly, he'd understand that I had to get the answers about my father's death. At least, he'd been patient with it so far.

By the end of the day, I'd heard back from Nathan. I felt disappointed when I learned that, because of our plans for the mining tour and the private investigator's busy schedule, the expedition to the warehouse would have to wait until after the new year. I found consolation by launching myself into the heap of paperwork back at home.

CHAPTER NINE

Finally, Saturday arrived with crystal-clear skies, the air crisp and cool as they drove toward the helicopter pad at Falcon Field airport. Libby was excited, her eyes gleaming as she chatted about the breathtaking views they were about to experience. Shadow stayed with Libby's sister for the day, freeing them up to enjoy a full experience without distractions. Libby looked over at Greg surprised when she realized they were the only two passengers.

"I thought you said…" she started.

He only smiled back.

Greg's anticipation grew, his hand occasionally brushing against the ring box hidden in his jacket. This time, nothing would go wrong.

The pilot greeted them warmly as they climbed into

the sleek helicopter, the blades already whirring above. Libby slipped on her headset, giving Greg a thumbs-up as the helicopter lifted into the air, the ground quickly falling away beneath them, leaving Mesa behind.

As they soared over the rugged terrain of the Four Peaks Wilderness, the landscape unfolded beneath them in a breathtaking array of colors—deep greens from the trees, brown cliffs, and veins hidden in the rock below. The mine property came into view ahead as they imagined glittering jewels embedded inside the mountainside.

"This is incredible!" she exclaimed over the headset. "You can see everything from up here."

Greg smiled, his nerves fading as he watched her excitement. The helicopter circled the mining site, giving them a stunning aerial view. Below, he could see the small operational camp, equipment lined up neatly. The sensation was like hovering over the heart of a mystery yet to be discovered.

This is it, Greg thought, his hand moving to the ring box in his jacket. The day couldn't have been more perfect— clear skies, the amethyst mine gleaming below them, and Libby's wide-eyed joy.

But just as he opened his mouth to speak, a sudden jolt rocked the helicopter. Greg felt his throat constrict as the aircraft shuddered, the nose dipping slightly.

"What was that?" Libby asked, her voice tight with alarm.

Greg glanced at the pilot, whose calm demeanor suddenly shifted. The man was scanning the controls, his expression serious. "Hold on, folks," the pilot said, adjusting the stick. "We've hit some turbulence—nothing to worry about, but I'm going to level us out."

The helicopter swayed again, and Greg's hand instinctively grabbed the side of the seat. The pilot regained control quickly, but the sudden tension had killed the moment. He couldn't propose in the middle of what felt like an emergency.

Libby's hand found his, squeezing it as she glanced nervously out the window. "Everything okay?" she asked.

Greg nodded, but inside, frustration simmered. Every time he thought he'd found the perfect moment, something went wrong. They passed over the mine once more, the helicopter now stable, but the magic of the moment lost.

The turbulence didn't ease. Instead, the shaking grew worse, and the pilot's calm demeanor shifted to alarm. Libby gripped Greg's arm tightly, her wide eyes meeting his as the helicopter jolted again, this time with more intensity.

"Folks, we've got us a mechanical issue," the pilot announced, his voice tense. "I'm going to set us down on the mountain. Hang on!"

He felt the ring box heavy in his pocket, but quickly forgot it as the helicopter rapidly descended. The wind whipped against the rotors, and with a hard thud, they landed on a flat stretch of rocky ground. Dust kicked up around them, and the engine sputtered before going silent.

For a moment, there was only the sound of their breathing, the uncanny stillness of the wilderness settling around them. Greg exchanged a glance with Libby, both of them still reeling from the shock.

"You okay?" Greg asked with concern, his voice shaky.

Libby nodded, though her face was pale. "Yeah ... I think so. What now?"

The pilot climbed out, assessing the situation. "I'm going to call for assistance, but it might be awhile before help arrives. We're pretty remote up here."

Greg surveyed the landscape. It loomed like a dark wound in the mountainside, the surrounding air colder and strangely still.

"We might have to hike for a bit if the weather turns," the pilot added, checking the radio. "I've got packs here with some provisions. There's an old miner's outpost nearby—we can always take shelter there."

Greg's gaze shifted to Libby. The strange things that had happened on their previous hike on this mountain rushed back into his thoughts. The proposal was long forgotten now, replaced by an unsettling feeling creeping over him.

"Well, this has sure turned into another adventure," Libby softly spoke, trying not to be heard by the pilot. "What is it with this mountain?"

As they waited for word from the helicopter company, the wind picked up, carrying with it an eeriness they'd experienced before. The pilot frowned at the darkening clouds and suggested they make their way to the miner's outpost, which was also near the mine entrance. Greg and Libby eagerly responded; anything to get out of the chilly wind.

They set off on foot, with their small day packs the pilot had provided, hiking toward the outpost. The trail was rough, with jagged rocks and narrow ledges overlooking steep drops. Every few steps, Greg felt the strange history of the place bearing down on them. This time, Shadow wasn't there to alert them to danger—it was only the two of them and their pilot navigating the terrain. Greg kept his eye on the pilot, too; he sensed something that caused him uneasiness. The guy had been nice enough, but there was just *something* that felt off.

As they neared a dilapidated structure, Libby stopped, her gaze fixed on something ahead. "Greg ... look."

At first, Greg didn't see it. But then he followed her gaze to the ground. What Libby was pointing at were the footprints—fresh ones. They weren't from animals—these were boot prints, deep and deliberate.

"Someone's been here recently," Libby whispered, a chill in her voice.

Greg's stomach tightened. He'd been told the mine was not in operation. The pitch he'd received was that they conducted tours with only small groups of people occasionally. And, from their own tour today, it appeared to be a poorly organized one, which made him wonder how often people came here.

The pilot caught up to them, squinting at what they were looking at. "That's odd," he muttered. "No one's scheduled to be up here today. Only the three of us."

That was the first time Greg noticed the pilot wasn't wearing a company uniform. No logo, no name badge on his flight suit. Although when they introduced themselves, he'd said to call him Pat. That's when it dawned on him the guy wasn't only their pilot. "You're our tour guide also?"

Pat nodded, then looked back in the direction from which they'd come, clearly uncomfortable about having left his machine unattended. In fact, he looked completely out of his element and not at all comfortable with the surroundings.

A low, scraping noise echoed ahead. The three of them froze. The sound all too familiar—metal against stone, like they'd heard on their hike before. Greg's pulse quickened.

"Did you hear that?" Libby asked, her voice tightened.

Greg quickly turned to look, with the memory of the

figure they'd seen during their previous hike—the miner, or whatever it was, who had followed them.

"Let's move," the pilot said, breaking the tension. "We'll head to the outpost, and I'll try to get a signal from there."

They continued their hike, but Greg couldn't shake the feeling that they were being watched. The farther they went, the more the mountain seemed to close in around them, the air growing colder and the sky darker. Shadows stretched across the trail, and every now and then, a scent wafted by that he couldn't identify.

By the time they reached the outpost near the mine entrance, the wind had picked up to a howling gale, and the temperature had dropped significantly. The outpost itself was little more than a wooden shack. The windows were broken, and the door creaked ominously as they pushed it open.

Inside, the air was thick with dust, and old rusted tools lay scattered about. Greg and Libby huddled together while the pilot fiddled with the radio, trying to get a signal.

Suddenly, a loud crash echoed from outside, followed by a low moaning sound. Was it the wind? It sounded—almost human, Greg thought.

"What was that?" Libby asked, her eyes widened.

Greg listened intently, looking through the broken-out window. The sound came again, only this time closer. Then, the scraping—metal against rock, like something being dragged.

"It's coming from the mine over there," Greg whispered, his stomach churning with dread. They both looked out to see the distinct entrance of the mine, very different from where they'd been the first time they visited the mountain trails.

Before anyone could react, the door burst open, and a small figure stood silhouetted in the entrance. It was hunched over, dressed in ragged, old-fashioned clothes, and holding a pickaxe. Its face was obscured by shadows, but the rasping breaths it took filled the room with an icy chill.

Greg froze, his eyes fixed on the figure as it stepped inside. He was certain it was the same one they had seen during their hike. Only now, it was closer—too close.

Libby gasped, stepping back instinctively. "Greg ... is that..."

Before she could finish, the figure dropped his pickaxe, causing a loud reverberation on the ground in the confined space. The pilot scrambled backward; his eyes filled with disbelief.

The figure stood still for a moment. Greg considered trying to grab for the pickaxe, but his feet felt rooted to the ground. Then, with a toothless smile, the ghostly miner stared directly at them. His eyes appeared friendly; the situation completely unsettling. The trio stared without blinking—watching him lift his long index finger, motioning for them to follow. Without a word, he turned and shuffled out of the building, pausing, and turned his gaze back to them. With a tilt of his head, he indicated again that they were to follow him.

"What ... what just happened?" Libby asked, her voice trembling.

"I don't know," Greg replied, but his gut told him they hadn't seen the last of the ghostly miner. "Did you see him pointing to the mine entrance?"

Libby nodded. "I think he was trying to tell us something. He wants us to follow him."

With frantic eyes, Pat stood there gawking at both of them. "Are you nuts? We've got to get out of here."

CHAPTER TEN

Greg, Libby, and the pilot stood in stunned silence as the figure slowly moved toward the mine entrance. The scraping sound echoed once more before fading into the depths of the cave.

"We need to go," Pat said, his voice shaky. "Now."

But Greg wasn't so sure. There was something about the ghostly miner's behavior that seemed to quiet his fear. The way he got their attention, insistently motioning for them. The rescuer in him knew they must act.

"I think we need to go inside," Greg said, his voice unwavering despite the adrenaline coursing through him.

Libby's eyes widened. "Are you serious?"

"We can't just leave without knowing what's going on," Greg insisted. "Something—*someone*—is in that mine.

And they've been trying to get our attention. You saw his expression—he needs our help." He pulled the small pack from his back, unzipped it, and started rummaging through. A flashlight, a water bottle, a hard hat with a headlamp, and some gloves.

Pat shook his head. "I'm not following that thing. You two can do what you want, but I'm going for help."

Greg and Libby exchanged a glance, the tension thick between them. Despite their fear and the danger, they both felt they needed to help. The mine held secrets, and it was time to face the mystery head-on.

Greg turned to the pilot, still considering which was scarier—the damaged helicopter or the mysterious mine. "Keep trying for a cell signal for help. We'll meet you at the helicopter. If you don't see us within an hour—send authorities to find us."

Then he turned to Libby. "In your bag—get that hard hat and those gloves on. I think you've also got a flashlight. Let's go."

Without hesitation, she followed Greg's instruction and then put the bag over her shoulders. "Let's go."

Taking a deep breath, Greg stepped toward the mine entrance with Libby close behind. The darkness seemed to swallow them as they crossed the threshold, the air thick with something far older—something ancient and restless, waiting for them in the shadows.

As Greg and Libby crossed into the amethyst mine, the daylight faded behind them, swallowed by the oppressive darkness of the cave. Their footfalls echoed unnaturally off the stone walls, the air cool and damp, filled with the faint scent of earth. Greg's headlamp flickered, casting long, wavering shadows against the rocky tunnel. He glanced back at Libby, who followed closely, her face set with determination despite the spooky atmosphere.

The deeper they went, the more the sense of being watched intensified. The mine was hauntingly quiet, almost as if the mountain itself was holding its breath, waiting for something to happen. Greg's thoughts went to that of the figure—the ghostly miner who had led them here, who had appeared again and again to them since that first encounter.

Libby broke the silence, her voice a whisper. "Greg, do you think … that apparition, that miner … do you think he's *trapped* here?"

Greg hesitated, considering her words. "I don't know. That, or someone else might be?"

Libby nodded, glancing warily around as they ventured deeper into the tunnel. The air grew colder, and they shone their flashlights around on both sides of the long passageway. Strange markings appeared on the walls— symbols carved into the stone, ancient and unfamiliar. Some looked like miner's tools, others more cryptic— spirals, jagged lines, and a series of interconnected circles.

"Did miners do this?" Libby asked, lightly touching the carvings.

"I don't think so," Greg replied, his voice low. "They seem much older than that, anyway."

As they continued, the tunnel widened, opening into an enormous cavern. Greg's headlamp illuminated the space, revealing veins of deep purple amethyst embedded in the walls, glittering with an almost supernatural light. But it wasn't just the crystals that caught their attention.

In the center of the cavern stood another old mining cart, tipped over and abandoned, its contents scattered across the ground. Among the debris were tools, rusted and forgotten, and something else—bones lying about, covered in dust.

Libby gasped, stepping back. "Greg ... look at this."

Greg knelt beside the remains feeling a tightness grip his chest. The bones were old, definitely not from recent mining activities. But why would they still be here at all? He took in the scene, glancing across the vast space. Then he saw it—a skeletal hand clutched something—an amulet of sorts, blackened with age but still intact, hanging from a tarnished chain. Greg carefully pried it loose, the metal cold against his skin. The pendant bore a few of the same strange symbols they had seen on the walls.

"What do you think this means?" Libby asked, her voice trembling

Before Greg could answer, a faint whispering sound echoed through the cavern, like the distant murmur of voices carried by wind. Greg and Libby both froze, turning toward the tunnel they had come from. The sound was growing louder, more distinct—multiple voices, layered over one another, speaking in a language neither of them understood.

Then, from the shadows, their coy apparition friend appeared again. This time, he was closer—much closer. Despite the darkness, the gaunt outlines of an older, overworked man became more visible on his face. The pickaxe rested in his hand, but now it seemed to glow faintly, as though infused with the light of the amethyst surrounding them.

Without thinking, Greg's fingers tightened around the pendant in his hand. "Who are you?" he called out, his voice echoing in the vast chamber.

The miner's figure remained silent for a moment before

raising his hand and pointing deeper into the cavern. The gesture was slow and deliberate, as though guiding them somewhere specific.

"We need to follow him," Greg whispered, feeling a pull he couldn't explain.

Libby hesitated, fear flashing in her eyes. "Are you sure?"

Greg nodded. "I think he's trying to show us something. Maybe it's about what happened here?" He pointed to the bones on the ground.

The miner led them through another narrow passageway, deeper into the heart of the mountain. The tunnel twisted and turned, descending sharply until they emerged into another vast chamber. But this one was different—more structured, more purposeful. Rows of old mining equipment throughout, and at the far end, they saw an enormous iron door embedded in the rock.

Greg's breath caught in his throat. The door was massive, reinforced with iron bars and heavy bolts. It looked like something of a fortress, completely out of place in a mine.

Libby moved closer to the door, inspecting the carvings that lined its surface. "These symbols—they're the same as the ones we saw earlier."

Greg nodded, studying the strange inscriptions. "This isn't just a mine. It has to be used for something else. But what?"

He stepped forward, placing his hand on the iron door. For a moment, nothing happened. He felt around and then the door began to creak and groan, the ancient mechanisms grinding as it slowly opened inward.

Beyond the door lay a room unlike anything they had

seen before. Shelves lined the walls, each one holding artifacts—ancient tools, jewelry, scrolls, as well as enormous geodes. But what caught Greg and Libby's attention was the large stone altar at the center of the room. On it lay a set of scrolls, bound with dark leather, the air around them thick with an energy that sent a shiver down Greg's spine.

"This must be it," Libby whispered. "Do you think this is what the miner was leading us to?"

Greg shrugged as he stepped forward, gently unrolling one of the scrolls. The language was unfamiliar, but the illustrations were clear—images of working miners, followed by scenes of death and despair. The final image depicted the amethyst mine itself, glowing with a strange light. Surrounding it were figures—human, but twisted and deformed, as if corrupted by something.

"It's a curse," Greg realized, his voice barely audible. "The mine ... it's cursed."

Libby's eyes widened. "What kind of curse?"

Greg studied the scroll more closely, as the pieces fell into place. "The people who worked here ... they weren't just digging for gems. There was something more to it."

"To what?" Libby asked, her voice trembling.

Before Greg could answer, the chamber trembled. The miner's ghostly figure appeared once more, standing at the entrance to the room. But this time, he wasn't alone. Apparitions swirled around him, forming the shapes of other miners—dozens of them, all trapped in the same twisted, ghostly form.

Greg's breath caught in his throat as he realized the truth. "They've been trapped inside here. Their spirits are bound to this place."

Libby's eyes filled with fear. "And if we don't get out ..."

we will be too."

The ground shook violently as the spirits of the miners moved toward them, their forms flickering like shadows in the dim light. Greg grabbed Libby's hand, pulling her toward the exit.

"I'm not sure what's happening, but we need to get out of here. Now!"

They sprinted out of the chamber, through the narrow passageway, the voices of the trapped souls echoing behind them. Feeling the tunnel closing in on them and hearing the walls vibrate with the force of the unleashed curse, Greg concentrated on how to get out. Hurriedly winding their way through the tunnels, Libby and Greg focused intently—one wrong turn, and they would be lost forever. When they crossed over the threshold and stepped out into the fresh air, the swirl of shadows rushed past, throwing them to the ground.

As they stood up again, dusting themselves off, they observed with wonder what looked to be a giant dust devil swirling away from the mine site. They turned around and the ghostly miner appeared at the entrance, standing silently just inside the threshold. He raised his hand, pointing once more—this time toward the pendant in Greg's hand. Where earlier he'd appeared faint—worn and haggard—now his image was powerful. His peaceful facial expression remained insistent as he continued to point toward the tarnished chain dangling between Greg's fingers.

Completely having forgot he still had it in his hand, recognition came to Greg. He understood what the miner was telling him. *It had been the key all along.* That hidden chamber, where the spirits were trapped, required the key to open it. The ghost took them to find that pendant and then led them to that hidden chamber. When they fled, thinking there was a curse, they were mistaken. The miner led them there not to trap them or harm them, but to set all those trapped spirits free.

As the last wisps of spirits faded, the ghostly miner stood before Greg, his gaze no longer filled with anguish but with the ease of quiet gratitude. Slowly, he extended his hand toward the pendant. Greg held it out, attempting to give it back. But instead, the miner nodded toward the artifact and then pointed at Greg's chest, indicating the treasure was his to keep.

Their spiritual friend held his gaze for a moment longer, then lifted his hand in a slow, sweeping motion, as if bestowing something beyond mere ownership: a blessing maybe, a promise of luck and fortune.

The miner suddenly vanished, and Libby looked at Greg with wide eyes, her voice hushed. "Greg ... you're meant to keep it."

Greg stared at the pendant, feeling its smooth, ancient surface in his hands. It felt different now, with a warmth he hadn't noticed before. Turning it over with his fingers, he saw something different from the old, lusterless metal he'd originally picked up. Now it shone beautifully and on the opposite side of those ancient symbols were gorgeous sparkling amethyst stones embedded that he hadn't noticed previously.

The wind had settled; no more tension in the air.

Greg stood wide-eyed, frozen in place. "What just happened?"

She silently and slowly shook her head in disbelief. "I-I'm not sure."

"Are you as spooked as I am?"

"Uh, huh. Yeah. We need to get out of here. Let's go find our pilot."

CHAPTER ELEVEN

On Tuesday, shortly before I was about to leave work for home, Nathan Pierce called me. It was time to visit that old abandoned warehouse where my dad had gone.

As I watched the traffic passing by, my mind shifted back to the weekend of ghostly encounters. I found myself having a difficult time getting back into detective mode. The whole experience was unsettling—if not downright otherworldly. Honestly, I wasn't sure what to make of it all. Ghosts? Trapped spirits? Greg and I are generally fairly open-minded, but how would we explain any of that to our friends? For now, we decided we shouldn't tell anyone. Who would believe us anyway?

Apart from that one strange encounter, I couldn't

figure out other parts of our journey. Everything from the organized 'tour' not happening as expected, then nearly crashing into the mountain, and, of course, the overall creepiness of the mine itself. Greg confided he had his suspicions about the pilot. I wasn't so sure about that, but I was so grateful Pat finally figured out the mechanical issue and got us home safely and without the need to hike back.

But this evening, I felt even happier to relegate myself to Nathan and ride along as a passenger on this latest excursion.

Nathan and I arrived at the edge of the industrial district just as dusk settled over the city, casting long shadows over the old, forgotten buildings. The warehouse loomed ahead, surrounded by a chain-link fence with patches of rust, a relic of a once-thriving business sector now abandoned. With broken windows, faded graffiti marking the outside walls, and dark shadows everywhere, this was the last place I felt we needed to be. *Why couldn't we have done this in the daylight?*

Nathan glanced at me, his expression grim. "Stay close and keep your flashlight low. We don't need to attract any unwanted attention."

We slipped through a gap in the fence and made our way to a side entrance. Nathan gave the door a gentle push, and it creaked open, revealing a dark, empty space. Our footsteps echoed as we stepped inside, the smell of dust and old machinery thick in the air.

I shone my flashlight around, illuminating remnants of a past life—crates, a few broken-down forklifts, and some rusted equipment scattered about. As we moved deeper into the warehouse, the temperature seemed to drop, and I could feel the hairs on my neck prickling.

"Are we sure this place is safe?" I whispered, my voice barely above a breath.

Nathan gave me a reassuring nod, but kept his gaze focused on the path ahead. "If there's anything to find, it's going to be in the main office."

We approached the office—a small room in the back, enclosed by cracked windows and an old metal door, which stood slightly ajar. Inside, the room looked as though it had been left in a hurry: filing cabinets were half-open, papers strewn across the floor, and a few broken chairs lay haphazardly by the walls.

Nathan stepped inside first, his flashlight scanning the room. I followed, curiosity peaking as I looked around. I noticed a large filing cabinet in the corner, its drawers labeled with faded stickers. Tugging one of the drawers open, I saw inside were files thick with dust, each stamped with Frontier Fidelity's logo. My heart skipped a beat. I'd seen the logo before—and thought I must have remembered it from my childhood. I rifled through folders, the pages spilling out.

"I wonder if these were records your father was looking through," Nathan muttered, leaning over to inspect the documents. "Look at this—claims marked with unusually high payouts, all involving properties owned by the same handful of people."

My eyes scanned across the room in disbelief. "If Fidelity still exists, why haven't they removed these files? Seems reckless."

"I'm not entirely sure they know they're here. This was a storage facility—I believe someone rented the space. I'm not sure who, though. Your dad?"

I sifted through the pages, my father's handwriting

visible in the margins. Words like *fraud* and *staged* were scrawled in bold letters next to certain case numbers. I felt a rush of anger and sadness as I read through them. My father had clearly been onto something big.

"Guess I'm surprised the storage company didn't remove their equipment and such. There are a lot of valuable items in this warehouse besides just files," I murmured.

Suddenly, we heard a faint sound—a shuffling noise, like footsteps. Nathan's head snapped up, his eyes narrowing. He gestured for me to turn off my flashlight, and we both froze, listening intently. The sound grew louder, moving closer.

I glanced at Nathan, who motioned for me to stay low. We crouched behind the filing cabinets, holding our breath as the footsteps drew nearer. Through a crack in the door, I saw a shadow pass—a figure creeping through the warehouse, its flashlight sweeping over the space.

I felt the tension radiating from Nathan as he kept his eyes fixed on the doorway. We waited, hardly daring to breathe, until finally, the footsteps faded and the figure disappeared into the shadows.

When the silence returned, Nathan let out a slow breath. "We need to get out of here—now. They must have security still monitoring this place."

I nodded, still clutching the documents we'd found. We moved swiftly but quietly toward the side entrance, retracing our steps through the dimly lit space. Just as we reached the door, a voice rang out from the far end of the warehouse.

"Who's there?"

We froze, exchanging a look. Without another word,

Nathan pushed me forward, and we bolted. Ducking through the gap in the fence and sprinting down the deserted street, we ran for our lives.

Only when we were a safe distance from the warehouse did we stop, leaning against a wall to catch our breath. Nathan looked at me, his face tense. "They know we're looking now. If there was any doubt before, it's gone. We have to move fast."

I glanced down at the papers in my hand. They were all we had, yet maybe, just maybe, they were enough to finally uncover the truth my father had risked everything for. Before my eyes left the pages I held, a chill moved through me. The logo resembled the markings we'd seen inside the mine.

* * *

I marched right to the kitchen, setting the papers down next to the boxes from Mom's house, pulling out another folder, and my jaw dropped. The Frontier Fidelity logo—it was a combination of the same interconnected circles and swirls we'd seen on the mine walls.

Greg walked into the room. "I thought I heard you come in. How was your day?" He came up and squeezed me from behind, resting his chin on my shoulder.

"Look at this—does it look familiar?"

"Frontier Fidelity?"

"The logo…"

"Hmm. Maybe. I've never heard of that company, though."

"It's the insurance company my father worked for. But, look here…" I pointed out the circles. "Don't they look just like the ones we saw in the mine?"

He picked up the paper and scrutinized. "I guess so. But really, couldn't those have just been circles—I mean, what's a logo without the name of the company?"

"Well, there's Nike. You instantly know the company name by seeing the swoosh."

"Ah, good point. I'm not sure this is the same, though." He kissed my neck.

"Ok, but how about those swirls we saw on the walls— those with these," I pointed again to the paper. "Identical."

"I guess so," he said, as he turned me around and kissed my lips this time. When he pulled away, he asked, "Are you hungry?"

"I am. What are you thinking?"

"Sushi."

"Sounds like a plan. Wanna have dinner on our own, or shall we call the Johnsons and see if they're interested in joining us?"

"Let's call our friends."

Dipping my salmon roll into the wasabi sauce, I was curious about what JJ had learned at the police station.

He filled me in. "I think we're onto something related to the Coronado fire, but what has really thrown me for a loop is how I've come across *many* heavily redacted key documents."

"That's not normal?"

"No. Also, witness statements taken at the time of the fire—nowhere to be found."

My eyebrows lifted as I consumed the roll and I blinked back the tears that sprung up from the hot wasabi. Quickly,

I took a drink of my water. "Is there anything else?" I asked with a scratchy voice.

"Well, yes. I've discovered there's one police officer's name in particular that keeps popping up in connection with the investigation—Detective Alan Ross. Multiple cases involving questionable payouts or ambiguous *accidental* deaths, where Frontier Fidelity provided coverage, link him, despite his spotless record on paper as a senior detective. They also listed Ross as one of the first responders on the scene when your father died, but there's no record of his official statement, though."

My stomach tightened.

"I've also been looking into Ross's digital footprint. I've uncovered emails between Ross and a senior agent at Frontier, Peter Daniels, discussing *settlement logistics* and *client protection*, with cryptic mentions of *mitigating risks*. The language is vague but suspicious, suggesting a back-and-forth about protecting clients and managing public perception after payouts."

Lexi poked JJ's side. "Tell them about the link with the amethyst mine."

Both Greg and I sat up a little straighter.

JJ took a sip of his wine. When he set his glass down, he stared directly at us. "This is where I probably really overstepped my bounds. I'm getting a little nervous about continuing with all this."

"Why?"

"Well, I found an expense report in Ross's email. It was an approved expense for remote security at an amethyst mine, coinciding with the timeframe of Libby's father's investigation into suspicious insurance claims. It is possible that someone assigned Ross the task of monitoring activities near the mine, potentially guarding the company's darker secrets. I mean, where better to bury evidence than inside a mine?"

Greg and I turned to each other; our faces paled.

CHAPTER TWELVE

Greg stepped out of his vehicle, looking at the exterior of the old-fashioned jewelry shop nestled in a quiet corner in Old Scottsdale, and his anticipation surged. The bell above the door chimed as he entered, and a man with wire-rimmed glasses looked up from his workbench, a welcoming smile on his face.

"Hello! Looking for something special?" the jeweler asked, setting down his loupe.

Greg nodded, slipping his hand into his pocket to pull out the pendant. He'd contemplated this decision ever since they came down off the mountain.

"I've got a bit of an unusual request," he said, glancing around the shop's cases of sparkling rings and necklaces. "I'd like to incorporate these amethyst stones into an engagement ring—a princess-cut diamond ring I already have. But only if you can preserve the pendant's integrity. I don't want it ruined—it's special."

The jeweler's eyebrows raised as he took the jewelry from Greg's hand, examining it with curiosity. "Beautiful," he murmured. "Quite old too, isn't it?"

Greg nodded, the memories of the mine echoing in his mind. "It's meaningful. Let's just say it has a lot of history." He glanced at the jeweler, feeling sheepish. "And I'd like the amethyst to be a part of my proposal to the woman I love. Kind of ... *a key to my heart*."

The jeweler seemed to sense the story left unsaid. With a gentle nod, he led Greg over to his workbench, where he placed the stones under the light. He picked up a pencil and sketched out a few ideas, capturing Greg's vision—a thin band of platinum around the existing princess-cut diamond with the amethysts set as a smaller stone on either side, cradling the diamond.

"How's this?" he asked, turning the sketch to face Greg.

Greg's breath caught; it was perfect. The amethysts seemed to blend seamlessly with the diamond, as if they had always been part of the ring, lending it a unique sparkle and warmth.

"That's it," Greg said, his voice thick with emotion. "It's exactly what I had imagined."

The jeweler gave him a reassuring smile, carefully removing the stones from its setting on the medallion and prepping them for their new home. "Give me a few days," he said. "And it'll be ready—just in time for you to ask her."

"And the pendant ... do you have suggestions? Maybe polish it? Will it look scarred where the gems are removed?"

"Oh, don't you worry. My specialty!" The kindly gentleman smiled. "You will love it."

Greg left the shop feeling a quiet thrill, knowing that soon Libby would wear not only a beautiful ring but one that carried their past and a promise of their future.

As soon as he started his truck, his phone rang—Libby.

"Hey, sweetheart. Whatcha up to?" she greeted.

He looked out his windshield, scanning around the parking lot, sure she had caught him red-handed.

"Oh, running errands. Are you still at work?" His eyes continued casing the area to make sure she wasn't ready to sneak up on him.

"I'm between appointments, outside walking Shadow. I just couldn't get it out of my mind—what JJ was saying last night."

"Which part?"

"Could there really be a connection to the amethyst mine? How coincidental would that be?"

"Yeah, I know what you're saying. It is fairly crazy that we discovered it—but then to keep hearing about it is unsettling. I'm not sure how, or if, it coincides. However, there could be a link simply because the mine was a policyholder at Frontier Fidelity."

"Yeah. And I'm not sure how that would be tied to the Coronado fire."

"Or if it is at all?"

"True. Anyway, I'll be a little later than usual. I'm meeting with Nathan again after work."

"How's that going?"

"Slow." She sighed as a display of her impatience.

"Want me to make dinner?"

"Oooh, I'd love that. Surprise me."

Greg grinned. He hung up and stopped by the grocery store on the way home. Steak, potatoes, and salad makings—his stomach growled already.

CHAPTER THIRTEEN

On my way over to Nathan's office, I felt a strange exhilaration—a sense of clarity in the search for my father's truth. Despite our last encounter at the warehouse, I was eager to discuss the case with him again.

"We have enough here to make some noise," I said, looking at Nathan across the desk.

He nodded. "It's a start, but we need more than just the documents. These names and connections ... well, they're a strong lead, but if we want to expose them, we'll need to find physical evidence that proves the claims were orchestrated. We need something irrefutable, and I think that's where your father had struggled."

My mind raced, thinking about what we could do next. "What about the people involved in the payouts? If we could talk to anyone who received a settlement, someone might have noticed odd behavior or strange demands from the company."

Nathan raised an eyebrow. "It's a bold move. But there's one person on this list that stands out." He flipped through the documents, stopping at a name scrawled in my father's handwriting—Rebecca Calhoun. "She owned a series of commercial properties that 'coincidentally' burned down one after another. Your father had marked her file with a question mark, as if he suspected she knew more than she let on."

"Do you think she'd talk to us?" I asked.

Nathan sighed. "If she's complicit, she'll deny everything. But if she's a victim, she might not understand she was being manipulated. It's worth a shot."

For the rest of the afternoon, we went over all the notes, developing a plan to approach Rebecca. Nathan suggested we pose as prospective investment business partners, a pretext that might lead her to let her guard down if she thought it was an opportunity to make a profit.

* * *

I opened the front door to the savory aroma of garlic and rosemary, and my senses were overloaded. Spotting Greg at the grill, expertly handling a sizzling steak, I dropped my bag on the counter and joined him on the patio.

"Smells delicious!" I leaned down to greet a boisterous black Labrador.

Greg turned, grinning as he flipped the steak. "Only the best for you. Thought we could have a cozy dinner tonight—just us and these beautiful steaks."

I gave him a peck on the cheek and offered to pour wine. By the time I'd freshened up and opened the wine bottle, he was back inside with two juicy steaks and a dog following diligently alongside. I took a seat, my stomach growling as I watched him plate the food, arranging everything with the care that made my heart melt a little more. I'm pretty sure Shadow agreed with that sentiment—her large brown eyes said so. Soon enough, he set a gorgeous spread in front of me: juicy steak, roasted baby potatoes, and a vibrant green salad on the side.

"This looks incredible, sweetie," I said, beaming up at him. "You're spoiling me tonight."

He shrugged, joining me at the table with his own plate. "You deserve it."

We clinked our glasses and dug into our meal, savoring each bite. The evening was quiet, warm, and everything I had been craving after a day full of questions. After we'd finished eating and were chatting over wine, a cheerful knock sounded at the door. My eyes flew open—I'd totally forgotten about game night. I gave my boyfriend a sheepish 'sorry' when I explained how I'd been so distracted that I forgot all about it.

Greg laughed and got up to answer the door. "Oh look! Friends!"

In walked Bella, carrying a shaker and cocktail glasses, with Brad and Cody right behind her, hands full of games. "Did somebody say game night?" Brad announced with a grin, glancing around. "And ooh, looks like we came just in time for the after-party! It smells delicious in here…"

I laughed, getting up to greet them with hugs. "Game night sounds perfect! What're we playing?"

Bella set her cocktail mixer on the counter, grinning. "I've got a special treat tonight—Cranberry Moscow Mules for everyone!"

Greg's eyes lit up as he helped Brad and Cody set up the games on the coffee table. "You two never let us down."

Brad laughed, draping an arm over Cody. "Oh, you know us. We never come unprepared. Cody's got Cards Against Humanity, and I brought Codenames and Uno Flip—it's time for some friendly competition!"

I grabbed the cocktails Bella had just mixed and handed them around. "To game night! And to Brad and Cody, for keeping us entertained!"

"To Brad and Cody!" everyone echoed, raising their glasses before taking the first sip.

As the night went on, the laughter was non-stop. Bella made up ridiculous rules for each round, sending everyone into fits of giggles, while Brad and Cody were in rare form, cracking jokes, doing impressions, and encouraging everyone to take risks with their game choices. Every now and then, Bella would jump up to refill everyone's cocktails, keeping the energy high.

By the time we'd made it to the final round of Codenames, I was wiping tears of laughter from my eyes, trying to breathe. Greg leaned over, grinning as he clinked his glass against mine. "I'd say this was a successful night."

"Absolutely," I replied, feeling a warm glow as I looked around at my friends.

* * *

The next afternoon, after I got off work, Nathan and I arrived at Rebecca Calhoun's upscale office building. We posed as a small development firm interested in learning how her investment strategies had helped keep her businesses afloat during difficult times. Rebecca was a charismatic, polished woman in her late fifties who welcomed us warmly. She seemed eager to discuss her business acumen, seemingly proud of the way she'd managed her properties.

As we spoke, I noted possible subtle discrepancies in Rebecca's story—details she claimed were because of good instincts, but that seemed less like luck and more about insider knowledge. Then she surprised us. She casually mentioned high settlement insurance payouts that allowed her to reinvest without ever suffering financial loss. *Was that good business acumen? I don't think so. There's definitely something to learn here.*

Nathan played along, pushing gently on certain points. "What insurance company are you with, by the way?"

"Oh, Frontier Fidelity takes great care of my investment properties."

Nathan smiled and leaned in, softly asking, "And those *reinvestments* you mentioned, sounds like you had an advantage there? Insider knowledge?"

Rebecca gave him a wary look. "Well, I don't know about that," she quickly added. "What makes you think I'm not a savvy investor in my own right?"

I leaned forward. "Sure, but those insurance payouts ... how'd that work?"

Rebecca's gaze flickered, just briefly. She shifted the conversation. "Could I get you both some coffee?"

Nathan nodded. I declined.

As Rebecca stood and walked across the room to pour the coffee, my eyes quickly scanned over the paperwork scattered across her desk. An envelope from Frontier

Fidelity sat in the far corner. Nathan nudged me when she finished pouring.

Rebecca shifted uncomfortably as she settled back in her seat. She sighed, frustration building in her voice. "It's complicated, to say the least. The policies were unusual, granted, but my agent handled everything. I really never had the need to ask any questions."

I shot Nathan a quick look. We both realized that Rebecca was not going to divulge much more. Nathan turned on his charm; he complimented her success and spoke of her reputation in the real estate investment community, as he sipped his coffee. I wondered if he actually knew these things about her, or if it was all a line of crap? He was good, though, I had to hand him that.

Mostly, as they talked, I found myself wanting to jump up and snatch the Frontier Fidelity envelope near her left elbow and run out of there. Of course, I didn't. I sat and listened, keeping attentive to her body language. Her jittery hands, bouncing knee, and a consistent twitch in her right eye—she was a nervous one, that was for sure.

Soon enough, Nathan had schmoozed her into recommending someone at Frontier Fidelity. She gave us the name: Peter Daniels.

After leaving Rebecca's office, we stopped for dinner. Nathan and I sat for a couple hours, piecing together our next steps.

"If this Peter Daniels arranged those payouts," Nathan said, "he's likely a key player in the fraud scheme. It sounds like he had a vested interest in Rebecca's claims—and probably others, too."

I made a note to look through the files at home, certain my father's handwriting marked Peter Daniels's name several times, each one underlined. I'd double check, but regardless, I stated, "He's the one we need to question next."

But Nathan's expression darkened. "If Daniels is as involved as we think, he won't just roll over. He might even get aggressive if he feels cornered."

I nodded, preparing myself. "Then we make sure he doesn't see us coming."

With Nathan's help, I was now ready to expose Peter Daniels and his connections to Frontier Fidelity. But we both knew we'd have to be cautious—our investigation had already put us in danger once, and approaching Daniels could put us in even greater risk. With a clearer picture of my father's investigation, I prepared for our next move, determined to uncover everything.

By the time I arrived home, Greg and Shadow were curled up on the sofa, fast asleep.

* * *

The early morning sun cast a warm glow over the desert as we jogged down the familiar path, Shadow trotting happily by my side. My thoughts wandered as my feet pounded the trail, but it always came back to Dad's notebook and the questions I still couldn't answer. I hadn't stopped digging, but as the days passed, each new piece of information only deepened the mystery.

Coming back into the neighborhood, we rounded the corner near the coffee shop, and Shadow nudged me, clearly hoping for a stop. Smiling, I slowed down, deciding a quick break wouldn't hurt. I looped Shadow's leash around the post by the entrance and ducked inside, my senses greeted by the rich aroma of freshly brewed coffee.

As I waited in line, I noticed the same guy Lexi and I befriended at the sushi bar was sitting by the window, nursing a latte and flipping through a stack of papers. *What was his name?* I waved, and he looked up, his face lighting up with recognition.

"Libby! What a surprise," he said as I approached. "Fancy meeting you here this early."

"Yeah, just out for a run with Shadow." I pointed to the black nose pressed at the window. "We can't resist a coffee stop afterward," I mentioned with a smile, but still struggling to remember his name. "How about you? Getting an early start on work?"

He shrugged, looking at the scattered documents around him. "Something like that. Just reviewing some records from the town's archives."

I nodded. "I remember you mentioning you were a historian. What kind of research are you doing?" *Now, if I could only remember his name!*

"Oh, I do a little bit of everything. The college keeps me busy," he replied, a bit evasively, then smiled as he sipped his coffee. "The stories hidden in this town's history would surprise you. It's what keeps me going."

I raised an eyebrow, pressing a bit. "So, does that mean you focus on local history, or do you do other kinds of work, too?"

He chuckled. "A lot of everything, actually. Local history mostly, but there's always something to learn. I have a curious mind that continually needs feeding."

I nodded, my curiosity piqued. "Sounds like fascinating work. I'd love to hear more about it sometime."

His face lit up, and he leaned forward. "Absolutely. In

fact, I still fully plan on booking my wife a massage. I got her that holiday gift card you were promoting. She's been talking about needing a break for weeks now."

"Send her my way! I'd love to meet her, and it's a great time to take advantage of the promotion."

He grinned. "Deal. And hey, maybe we can arrange another sushi night soon—this time with our significant others. I know Rob's been wanting to hang out again, too."

It suddenly hit me. *Ah, Rob and Tony—his name is Tony!*

"That sounds great," I replied, nodding. "Greg and I would be up for that, and I'll see what Lexi and her husband are up to." I paused, choosing my next words carefully. "What exactly does Rob do again?"

He hesitated, glancing down at his coffee before looking back up. "Uh, investment banking; he's a consultant. He's worked with a few businesses around here, just helping them with their records and financials, you know?"

I smiled, filing away the details. "Interesting. Well, I'll let you get back to your work. Enjoy your coffee, and I'll look out for your wife at the spa!"

CHAPTER FOURTEEN

Nathan and I stepped into the upscale lobby of Frontier Fidelity Insurance, where sleek marble floors and wood accents set the tone. We made our way to the receptionist, who led us to Peter Daniels's office. He greeted us with a polished smile, a shining example of corporate charm, his sharp suit and confident posture almost intimidating.

"Libby," he said warmly, extending a hand. "I knew your father well—a good man, dedicated to his work."

I managed a polite smile to go with the handshake, but felt his warmth was hollow. "I'd like to believe he dedicated himself to finding the truth."

Nathan nodded, also firmly shaking his hand. "We were hoping you might help us fill in some gaps. We found

Leon was investigating some unusual insurance claims before his passing—specifically, properties with frequent, high-payout claims."

Daniels's eyes darkened, but his expression remained neutral. "Those claims were all fully investigated, I assure you. Frontier Fidelity prides itself on maintaining a thorough and transparent process."

I looked at him directly and lied slightly. "My father noted some cases involving an amethyst mine—claims associated with it, actually, but we haven't found any obvious answers about what he was working on out there."

Daniels shifted in his seat, but his smile never wavered. "Ah, the mine. Yes, it's an old site—both historic and somewhat risky. Not a lot of work goes on there now. But I'm curious: why is your interest in the mine?"

Nathan exchanged a look with me, measuring our next move. "Well, for one, we'd like to understand the need for private security—considering, as you say, there's no mining activity going on. Also, it looks like Leon questioned some high insurance payouts on the surrounding land. That doesn't quite add up, especially given its supposedly low activity."

Daniels chuckled, a dry, calculating sound. "You have to understand, the mine is valuable not just in terms of its history but also real estate. Many high-net-worth individuals have interests in rare minerals and mining properties."

He leaned back, hands steepled as if pondering something. "I tell you what—I have a property inspection scheduled out there later this week. It's mostly a formality, but if you'd like, I could arrange a visit for you both. I think seeing it might clear up any suspicions." His smile seemed almost too smooth; his eyes appraising.

I nodded, playing along. "That would be helpful,

actually. I've always been curious about the place."

Daniels nodded, satisfied. "Excellent. It's only accessible by helicopter. Well, unless you're up for the arduous hike—I'm sure not." He chuckled, patting his sizeable waistline. "But I'll send directions to our helipad once we've settled on a time. You'll see it's simply an old, mostly unused property. Nothing mysterious about it at all."

When we left his office, I turned to Nathan, my thoughts racing. "Did you hear him say 'mostly unused'? And he didn't blink once at the idea of us visiting it." I left out the part where I've already been inside the mine. But it got me thinking about whether the pilot would recognize me. *Would it be the same pilot?*

Nathan nodded; his jaw tight. "If he's willing to take us there, it's because he thinks he's in control—he only wants us to see exactly what he wants. We'll need to stay on our guard. There's no telling what he might be trying to hide."

After thinking that through, I agreed. It appeared we both understood that the mine wasn't only an old property. Daniels had something to prove—or something to keep buried—and he intended to show us only what he wanted us to see.

Later that evening, I filled Greg in on the meeting details with Nathan and Peter Daniels. I noticed his expression shift from concern to intrigue as I recounted how Daniels had casually invited us to inspect the mine.

"So, Daniels just offered to take you there?" Greg asked, his eyebrows knitting together. "And you're actually going?"

I nodded. "He wants us to think it's a harmless inspection. But that he's taking us directly there makes me think even more that he's trying to cover up something. I'm interested in what he'd actually show us."

Greg folded his arms, studying me carefully. "I take it you haven't told him we'd already been inside the mine?"

I shook my head.

"How are you going to explain if Pat is your pilot?"

"Hadn't really thought about that yet. Play it by ear?"

His expression turned to concern. "I'd prefer you didn't go alone with these men you hardly know."

I smiled wryly, hearing that hint of frustration in his voice. "Actually, Nathan and I discussed that. It would be much better if you were there, too. We could use another person on our side and with your skills, you'd notice things I might miss."

Greg raised an eyebrow, his skepticism melting into a half-smile. "So, you need a trained wilderness expert, huh?"

I grinned, reaching for his hand. "Exactly. If we both go, it might take Daniels off guard, which could work to our advantage."

Greg squeezed my hand, then glanced off thoughtfully. "Well, we know the terrain around the mine. It's remote, and there's barely any cell reception. If something goes wrong, we'll need to be prepared." He looked back at me, his expression growing serious. "But you're right—it's the best shot we have. I'll go with you."

Relief washed over me. "Thank you for understanding, sweetie. I know it's risky, but if we stick together, we'll have a better chance of finding out the truth."

He nodded, his gaze intent. "Then it's settled. And if Daniels has anything to hide, we'll figure it out."

Shadow barked and pawed at my leg.

"Oh, I'm sorry sweet pup. I'm not sure how to take you along…"

Greg gave Shadow some extra love, too, before coming over and embracing me. I hugged him tightly, reassured by his strength and commitment. Another trip to the mine was an added leap into spooky territory, but with Greg and Nathan by my side, I felt more prepared than ever to confront whatever truths were waiting to be unearthed. It was evident my father had questioned the operations and the related claims. I couldn't help but wonder whether our phantom miner would make an appearance.

The next day, I met JJ at a quiet café near his precinct, carefully choosing a seat in the back corner where we'd be less likely to be overheard. I filled him in on Daniels's invitation to the mine, watching his expression shift from curiosity to deep concern.

"You're seriously planning to fly out there with Daniels?" JJ asked, leaning in and lowering his voice. "You don't even know him. Libby, that's a high-stakes move. If Daniels has anything to hide, being in a remote location with him might be exactly what he wants—especially if it means controlling what you see."

I nodded, acknowledging the risk. "I know, JJ. But with Nathan and Greg both there, I seriously don't think he'll try anything stupid. He simply wants to take us there, say 'nothing to see here, folks', and then have us drop it."

JJ smirked.

"Unless there's more about Daniels, or this investigation, you'd like to fill me in on?"

JJ took a deep breath and glanced around, considering how much he should reveal. "Okay, look, I dug a little deeper into Peter Daniels. Turns out, Daniels has been under quiet suspicion for years *with the police force*. But nothing sticks to him apparently, and I think that's because he's careful and calculating—he's meticulous about keeping his hands clean."

He leaned forward, his voice barely above a whisper. "There's also a rumor floating around that he's connected to something bigger than insurance fraud. Apparently, he's got ties to some real estate deals and investment properties owned by high-profile people—clients of Frontier Fidelity. And, get this: several of these clients have 'protection agreements' with Frontier, meaning *damage control*."

"So, he's not just covering up a few claims. This is an entire network of shady payouts and cover-ups—maybe even some intentional 'accidents.' But how is the mine connected, I wonder?"

JJ nodded, his face tense. "Well, until this meeting, I hadn't considered the mine property. And if Daniels has brought in Detective Ross, or anyone else in the department, then he's got more than just corporate power behind him. He's got local law enforcement working to keep things under wraps. That must mean the stakes are high."

He paused, choosing his next words carefully. "Libby, you need to be ready for anything. I'll be monitoring Daniels's activities from here, and if you're flying to the mine, I'll keep track of that flight."

I felt a wave of gratitude. "Thank you, JJ. It's good to know you're looking out for us. I promise we'll stay cautious and watch for anything suspicious. We'll gather as much information as we can without tipping Daniels off."

JJ nodded; his eyes were deadly serious. "I can't help but think that you three are walking into something huge. Whatever you find out there, remember, Daniels plays dirty. He'll do whatever it takes to stay one step ahead, and if he thinks you're onto his operation, he might turn this trip into something dangerous."

I took a calming breath, knowing the risks, but also feeling more certain than ever. "We're ready, JJ. If this mine trip is the key to uncovering what really happened to my father, we'll take it. And yes, we'll be careful. I promise."

JJ reached across the table, giving my hand a quick squeeze. "Just don't underestimate him. And when you get back, we'll figure out what to do next. Promise me you'll call as soon as you land."

I smiled gratefully. "I promise."

CHAPTER FIFTEEN

Upon entering my mother's newly restored kitchen, we were greeted by the comforting scent of her famous lasagna and garlic bread, which had been freshly baked. The kitchen gleamed under the new, bright lights. The countertops were spotless, with a few playful touches she had added to celebrate the completion of repairs—a bright orange vase of sunflowers and a new stack of mismatched but charming dinner plates.

My sister, Jordan, was already there, setting the table with my nieces and nephews, Apple, Annie, Chase, and Ryan helping—or at least, trying to help. Apple was concentrating hard, arranging forks and spoons with a sense of perfectionism, while Annie darted around, leaving the napkins on each plate haphazardly. Chase and Ryan, meanwhile, were more preoccupied with Shadow, who was happily soaking up the attention from both, her tail wagging enthusiastically.

As we gathered around the table to eat, I leaned over to Jordan, asking how things had been since we last spoke. Jordan rolled her eyes with a good-natured smile. "Oh, you know, the usual," she said. "Apple's been into baking lately; ever since the Thanksgiving cooking sessions, she's *obsessed*. She's mastered banana bread, but now wants to bake a full-on cake, from scratch, for our next family event. I'm both impressed and slightly terrified."

I laughed, giving Apple an encouraging nod. "Banana bread sounds amazing—maybe you can teach me!"

My niece grinned proudly. "I'll make sure to bring you some next time!"

Annie piped up next, twirling a loose strand of her hair. "I've been practicing for the school play. I'm a tree. Well, not just a tree—a *singing* tree." She threw her hands up in a dramatic pose, earning laughs from everyone.

"Ah, so we have a future star here!" Greg said, giving her a high-five across the table.

Chase, now tugging on Shadow's ears, chimed in, "And I'm starting soccer next week!" He said with a competitive glint in his eyes. "Mom says we can't tackle," Chase added, rolling his eyes in a way that made everyone laugh.

As the conversation continued, I glanced around, feeling that sense of comfort and warmth I hadn't realized I'd missed. Mom beamed, watching her daughters and grandchildren fill the room with energy. This was exactly what she'd wanted her repaired kitchen to become—a hub of family, laughter, and little everyday stories.

Later, after our bellies were full, the family settled into

the living room with mugs of hot chocolate. Jordan and I lingered for a bit in the kitchen, where the kids wouldn't overhear the more serious parts of the conversation. I took a deep breath, glancing at my sister.

"Jordan," I began quietly, "I found some things out about Dad's passing that don't exactly add up."

Jordan's face softened, a mixture of curiosity and worry. "Already? What do you mean?"

I explained what I'd recently uncovered, hinting at the possibility that our father's job as an insurance adjuster might have put him at risk. Jordan listened intently, nodding, her expression growing more serious as I described the plan to go back to the amethyst mine with Greg and Nathan to dig deeper—quite literally—into the investigation.

"I think that place might hold some answers. Maybe even something connected to what happened to him," I said, my voice thick with a blend of conviction and lingering grief.

Jordan took my hand, giving it a reassuring squeeze. "Libby, I can't tell you how grateful I am that you're taking this seriously. I just *know* there's more than what we've been told. You have to see it through. Just be careful. And if you need anything…"

I nodded, feeling bolstered by my sister's support. "Yes, of course. Promise."

We returned to the living room, where the kids were now animatedly trying to entertain Shadow with treats they'd snuck from grandma's doggie cookie jar. Chase, noticing our serious tone as we walked in, jumped up. "What were you talking about?"

I exchanged a quick glance with Jordan, then grinned, deciding to turn my investigation into a story the kids would enjoy. "Well, you know how Greg and I went hiking up at the old amethyst mine?"

The youngest boys, Chase and Ryan, lit up with excitement. Even the teenagers, Apple and Annie, leaned in closer, eager for the details.

"Turns out," I continued, lowering my voice in a conspiratorial whisper, "that mine has a secret. They say it's guarded by the ghost of an old miner who watched over the mine for years and years."

Annie gasped, putting a hand to her mouth. "A real ghost?"

"Yup," I said with a wink. "But he's not a scary ghost. He's more like a helpful guide, making sure anyone who goes up there is safe and that the secrets of the mine stay protected."

Apple, always the thinker, tilted her head thoughtfully. "Sooo … does he, like, help you find treasure?"

I smiled, nodding. "Sort of. He's there to make sure the mine's treasures don't end up in the wrong hands. And if you're respectful and listen closely, he might just show you the way."

Jordan, catching on, added, "So you'd better believe that if Aunt Libby sees him, she'll ask him for all his best mining tips!"

The kids laughed, imagining the ghostly miner with a pickaxe and a glowing lantern leading the way. I leaned back, glad I'd shared just enough with my family while leaving a little magic in the air.

After sharing ghost stories, the kids' excitement carried over, and they begged Jordan and me to play a game of flashlight hide-and-seek in the backyard, inspired by the friendly ghost miner tale. Mom and Greg stayed inside with their mugs of coffee, watching from the warm glow of the kitchen window as we led the kids outside.

The crisp evening air filled with laughter as the kids dashed around, flashlights flickering, trying to find each other behind trees, bushes, and Julia's garden shed. Shadow joined in, trotting after them with her nose to the ground, helping them by finding all their hiding spots.

At one point, I crept up behind Apple, who was peeking out from behind a bush. "Boo!" I whispered, and Apple squealed, laughing and calling for backup as Chase and Ryan came running over to rescue her from the pretend ghost miner.

When everyone was finally found, we gathered in a huddle, out of breath and giggling, under the faint glow of moonlight. Jordan pulled her jacket tighter and suggested we head back in for dessert.

"How about some ghostly cupcakes?" she teased, referring to their grandma's snowmen dessert with white frosting and chocolate chip faces.

As they came inside, shaking off the cold and chattering about the game, I noticed Greg and Julia huddled near the kitchen counter, speaking in low voices. They were so engrossed in conversation that neither of them looked up right away, and it piqued my curiosity.

Shadow trotted past them toward her water bowl, and the kids piled into the living room, but I paused near the doorway, wondering if I should make my presence more known.

Mom glanced up first and caught my eye, her expression shifting from serious to warmly surprised. "Oh, Libby! We were just … uh, talking," she said, straightening up and giving Greg a look of subtle encouragement.

My gaze drifted to Greg, with his sheepish smile. "It's nothing serious, just, uh … planning for our upcoming venture, you know," he said, quickly recovering.

But something in his expression told me there was more. I watched my mom pat Greg's arm, clearly signaling that she'd leave us to it, then she walked over to the kids in the living room, calling them to go wash up in the bathroom. With the kitchen suddenly quiet, I stepped closer to Greg, my curiosity outweighing my hesitation.

"Upcoming adventure plans, huh?" I teased gently, raising an eyebrow. "Anything I should be concerned about?"

Greg's shoulders relaxed, and he chuckled softly, rubbing the back of his neck. "Alright, you got me. I … I was actually just asking your mom for some advice on a big decision I've been working up the nerve for."

My pulse quickened as nerves washed over me. "Oh? And what did she say?"

"She told me to follow my instincts and not overthink things," Greg said, meeting my eyes with a look that was both confident and affectionate. "And, well, I think my instincts have been telling me for a while now what the right answer is."

I felt warmth spread through me as I took his hand. The hint of something big, something exciting, lingered between us, but we both seemed content to leave it unsaid for now, savoring the moment and the unspoken promise it carried.

Just then, my mom reappeared with a wink, nudging us toward the dessert table. "Come on, you two! There's cider and cupcakes waiting, and we've got enough sweet stuff here to fuel another round of hide-and-seek."

I gave Greg's hand a quick squeeze, feeling a thrill of anticipation as we joined the rest of the family, knowing that whatever Greg's big decision might be, it was going to be worth the wait.

The family warmed up around the dining table with hot apple cider and snowman cupcakes, laughing as they recapped each hiding spot and every close call from the game. It was a simple night, filled with family, laughter, and a bit of magic—a reminder that despite the mysteries I was pursuing, I had a strong and loving family at my side, ready to support me through anything.

CHAPTER SIXTEEN

My phone rang early the next morning, the display showing Nathan's name. I answered quickly, my excitement from the night before now laced with a sense of caution.

"Hey, Nathan," I greeted. "What's up?"

There was a pause on the other end before he spoke. When he did, his voice was tight with concern. "I just heard from Daniels. He canceled our trip to the mine."

Shocked, I sat down. "What? Why?"

"Get this," Nathan replied, his tone edged with frustration. "He said there has been some 'unexpected site maintenance.' Claimed that safety inspections flagged 'unstable conditions' at the mine and that it's too risky to go there now. Said he'd have to reschedule the visit—no clear date, just 'sometime in the future.'"

I let the silence sit between us for a moment. "So … he's suddenly concerned about safety? Seems awfully convenient, don't you think? He never intended to take us there—it was all a ruse."

"Exactly," Nathan said with a sigh. "Or, it's a classic stall tactic. Either he realized we're onto something and doesn't want us anywhere near the mine, or he's buying himself time to clean up whatever he doesn't want us to see."

I gripped the phone tighter. "By that, do you mean he could be planning to get rid of any evidence that could be there?"

"Wouldn't be surprised," Nathan replied grimly. "If he suspects we're closing in, he'll do everything he can to sanitize that site. It could even mean he's got something lined up to get rid of any sensitive documents or, worse, to make the area completely inaccessible to us."

Trying to keep my frustration at bay, I exhaled. It had me wondering whether Daniels learned about our previous excursion to the mine. Ever since our trip up there, I'd wondered how Greg arranged that—with no active mining operations or personnel around. Something seemed fishy.

"So, what do we do now? Waiting around won't help, and who knows what Mr. Daniels is doing out there in the meantime?"

"We still have options," Nathan said thoughtfully. "His reaction alone gives us something to go on—it's practically an admission that there's something worth hiding. Maybe we don't need the official tour. What if we look into the mine's inspection history? I know a few people who can discreetly pull site records. We might see if these so-called 'safety issues' even exist."

I felt a surge of confidence. "And maybe we go check out the area ourselves, without Daniels watching our every move. We don't need him to tell us what to look at."

"Uh," Nathan's voice grew concerned. "Well, I suppose that means hiking in. Of course, you and Greg are capable of doing that; at my age, I'm not." He hesitated a moment. "For certain, you'd have to time it carefully to avoid attention. If you're lucky, you might find exactly what he's trying to hide."

A feeling of hope flickered. "I'll discuss it with Greg. If Daniels wants to keep us away, that's all the more reason we need to get out there."

We both knew we were treading on dangerous ground, but there was no turning back now.

Later that day, Greg and I sat at the kitchen table, poring over details of our previous helicopter tour, the one where we'd encountered strange turbulence which forced an emergency landing. My mind buzzed with questions—especially after hearing Nathan's reservations. I couldn't shake the feeling that someone may actively try to prevent us from getting too close to the truth.

I leaned forward, my voice hushed but intense. "Greg, I know this sounds paranoid, but could our previous flight have been more than just bad luck? Do you think it's likely that someone planned for us to have an accident up there?"

Greg nodded, his eyes narrowing as he considered it. "Who? Who even knew we booked that tour?" He stood and went to the refrigerator for a beer.

"Yeah, I don't know."

"I mean, I'm not saying you're wrong. The whole thing

was strange. I tell you what—I'll reach out to the number I called before and see what I can learn."

An hour later, after a few calls and some explaining, Greg got the information for the helicopter pilot who had flown them out there that day. His name was Pat Gannon.

When Greg spoke to him over the phone, he noticed Pat's tone was guarded at first. But once Greg explained he was trying to figure out more about the strange mechanical issue that had occurred, Pat's voice softened.

"Look, I don't know if you'll believe me," Pat began, "but that flight was … well, it was unusual, even for me. A company hired me as an independent contractor for a one-time deal. A consultant briefed me just before I flew you two out. He showed me the exact route to take and where to show my passengers a particular thrill ride. He actually directed me to act as if we were stranded. I thought it was odd, but they offered a big bonus to cover any damages if something went wrong."

Greg and I exchanged uneasy glances.

Pat continued, "I'm sorry if this sounds sketchy, but I swear, I thought it was just some high-paying customers wanting the thrill of flying over those tall cliffs. The way he made it sound, it almost seemed like one of those reality shows. Honestly, I didn't know it would shake the aircraft that hard. And then, the whole thing with the ghost—that was over-the-top. Whooo-weee, that scared the bejeezus outta me! When I got back to the aircraft and called in, I told them they'd gone too far. Of course, they had no idea what I was talking about."

Confused, I cut him off. "That was all *planned*?"

Pat sighed.

Greg wasn't satisfied. "What about this consultant?

What was his name?"

After a pause, Pat muttered, "Yeah. He said his name was Peter Daniels. I thought he was part of the mining company's management team."

I guess I hadn't fully understood what he had told us earlier. "You mean, you're *not* part of the mining company?"

"Oh no. Just the pilot hired for the day."

Greg cut in again. "And that's the only time you've flown for this company?"

"Yep."

Pieces of the puzzle were clicking into place, only I was having a difficult time getting them all in order. Daniels had set up the helicopter trip, planning every part of the route to put us at risk right near the mine site. It was almost as if he'd orchestrated the accident to scare us off—or worse. *But how did he even know us?* In his office this week, he never let on he knew me or that he knew I'd already been out to the mine.

After we ended the call with Pat, I stared at Greg, my voice shaking with anger. "Daniels knew us from our first hike up the mountain. Was it him in the forest—or that apparition? It was too hard to see." I stood up from the table and started pacing the kitchen. "Then when you called that number to inquire about a tour, he wanted to..." I couldn't even finish my horrible thought. "Question is— *how'd he know it was us?* I only met him this week. You were the one who called the company for the mine tour. And why on earth would an insurance executive be scheduling helicopter tours to the mine?" I was so confused.

Greg clenched his fists, the fortitude showing in his expression. "If Daniels went to that length to keep us away, then the mine must hold exactly what we're looking for. If we go back, we're going on foot—without him knowing."

I nodded. "Exactly."

My phone rang—JJ.

"Hey, my friend," I answered. "You'll never guess what we just learned."

"Oh yeah. Well, I've got one for you as well. Can I come over?"

"Of course. See you in a few."

Sitting at the table across from us, JJ's expression was tense, and I could tell he had something big. He wasted no time getting to the point, lowering his voice even though we were in a private setting.

"Libby," JJ began, "I managed to dig up some details about Detective Ross that tie him directly to Daniels. It's even bigger than I thought."

I leaned in. "What did you find?"

"Remember, Ross was the lead investigator on that fire—the Coronado Fire. Officially, it was declared an accident. But what I found in the department's files shows a massive payout from Frontier Fidelity Insurance to a shell company associated with Ross. It was a six-figure sum. Guess who signed off on that insurance claim?"

My eyes widened. "Peter Daniels."

JJ nodded grimly. "Exactly. I could piece together that Daniels approved the payout to the shell company, which Ross himself had actually set up. The money went through a series of transfers before disappearing into what looks like Ross's personal account. It's a huge conflict of interest."

The implications sank in. "So, Daniels and Ross worked

together to cover up the fire, and they used the payout to keep each other quiet. Daniels could have pressured Ross to classify the fire as an accident, knowing he'd benefit personally from it. And it means they could have been doing this for years, using similar methods."

Greg shook his head. "There has to be someone else involved. The fire department would be the ones who declare whether the fire was an accident. Ross certainly could alter documents, though."

JJ nodded. "True. There's more to discover for sure, but Daniels's role in Frontier Fidelity allowed him to handle high-value claims personally. If a fire or accident was suspicious, but valuable to the company or someone with ties to it, he could funnel money in and out of the company under the guise of 'claims,' making everyone involved richer."

I swallowed, anger simmering beneath the surface. "So, my dad's death—whatever he found out—could have been connected to this. Maybe he uncovered something about the fraud and Daniels's role in it, and Daniels needed him out of the way."

JJ's fists clenched. "I'd say there's a strong chance. Daniels has been running a cover-up operation, with Ross and maybe others in the department involved. It's looking more and more like your dad stumbled on something that made him a liability."

I took a shaky breath. "Thank you, JJ. If Daniels and Ross think they can scare us off, they're wrong. We're getting to the bottom of this."

Then JJ remembered. "Oh wait. You said you had something you'd learned?"

I paused only a moment, carefully considering the

connections between everything. Slowly, I explained our findings: how Greg and I had learned about Daniels's helicopter tour setup, his suspicious behavior bailing on his offer of a mine tour, and the terrible possibility that all of it could be connected to my father's death. JJ listened intently, his face darkening as I spoke, until suddenly, a flash of realization crossed his face.

"Libby," he interrupted, his voice low. "I just remembered something else. About a year ago, Ross filed a report about finding remains at the mine."

A tingle slithered down my spine. "Remains? You mean human remains?"

JJ nodded, his jaw tight. "Yeah. He classified it as 'unsolved' and reported the bones as historical finds, which put them under the jurisdiction of the state archaeologists instead of the police. It was strange at the time, but since they were in an old mining area, no one questioned it. But now I'm thinking those remains might not be as old as he made them out to be."

I felt a chill run down my spine. "You think they could be more recent—maybe even part of this cover-up?"

JJ's face grew even grimmer. "I mean, it's possible. Especially if Daniels or Ross wanted to hide the identities. Consider this: if people disappeared, or were murdered, to conceal this fraud, the mine could have served as a burial site. Declaring the bones 'historical' would be the perfect way to keep it quiet."

My thoughts whirled. "So, Daniels and Ross might have been using the mine not just to hide their fraud, but as a literal graveyard for anyone who got in the way. And my dad ... if he was onto their scheme, he could have ended up there too."

JJ reached across the table, taking my hand for support. "Libby, I think you're right. If Daniels has been using the mine for more than just fraud, your father might have discovered evidence of these 'disappearances' and how they connected to Frontier Fidelity claims."

"Then we have to go out there, JJ. Whatever hides in that mine, it's time we bring it all to light."

"I don't think any of us have enough money to hire a helicopter." JJ sat back in his chair.

Greg leaned in. "It's not *that* grueling of a hike. Libby and I drove to the trailhead, camped there, and then set out to the mine the next day. Now we know the most direct route there. It'll take us a couple days—there and back. But it's certainly doable."

JJ scratched his chin, thinking. "It seems risky."

I smiled at my friend, knowing one way to get him onboard. "Lexi was disappointed that she missed out the first time. Let's all go and make it an adventurous weekend."

The worry etched on JJ's face broke when he let out a pent-up breath. "Let me talk to Lexi. I'm not sure we can get away this weekend. I'm assuming that's when you're talking of going?"

We both nodded our heads.

"Let me see what I can do."

CHAPTER SEVENTEEN

I tried to cover all our bases before our trek to the mine. Knowing that Daniels was framing the mine as a protected historical site to keep people away, we needed hard evidence to counter those claims. I had a hunch Tony, the historian I'd met at the sushi bar, might be a good source of information.

The next day, I reached out to the community college, and after a few calls, I got Tony on the phone.

"Hey, Tony! It's Libby. I'm not sure you'll actually remember me, but we met at Satori Sushi? We also briefly talked at the coffee shop recently."

After a moment's pause, he replied warmly, "Libby! Of course, I remember. To what do I owe the pleasure?"

"I need some help researching an old mine," I

explained. "I've heard that it's been deemed a historical site and thought you might point me in the right direction to verify that information."

Tony sounded intrigued. "I'd be happy to help. There's a lot of lore around old mines in the area. If you can give me the name, I'll dig into what we have in the archives and see if there's anything significant about it."

I quickly filled him in, mentioning its history as an amethyst mine. Tony paused thoughtfully. "This doesn't ring a bell in terms of historical significance, but I'll confirm. And, if it is being used as a cover, there may be telltale gaps or alterations in the record."

"That's what I'm hoping to find out. And Tony— thanks. This means a lot."

"I'll get back to you as soon as I have something," he promised.

My phone buzzed. Seeing Nathan's name on the screen, I answered immediately, my pulse quickening. Shadow let out a bark and I realized I hadn't taken her out in hours.

"Nathan, hey—any updates?" I asked, as I punched the button. I strapped on Shadow's harness and leash and we headed out the front door.

Nathan's voice was tense, barely above a whisper. "Libby, I just got word from a contact I've been keeping tabs on. It sounds like Peter Daniels has gone off the radar. His office sits empty, someone disconnected his phone, and no one at Frontier Fidelity has seen him since yesterday."

"Wait, he's gone? Just like that?"

"Yep. And it gets weirder," Nathan continued. "Apparently, there was a sudden withdrawal of a huge sum from one of his accounts. No one knows where he is or what he's planning. But from the looks of it, I'd say someone tipped Daniels off that we're getting closer to the truth."

I closed my eyes, trying to process the implications. "So, he knew we were planning to go to the mine, maybe even that we've connected him to the fraud. He's running to keep ahead of us."

"Exactly," Nathan said grimly. "If he's disappeared, he might try to cover his tracks permanently—or worse, set up some kind of final sabotage to protect himself. I'd be cautious about that mine trip. We don't know what he might have done out there."

My jaw clenched, anger welling up. "We're going to that mine, Nathan. He's been a step ahead of us, but this time we're not letting him get away."

Nathan's voice softened. "I know you're determined, Libby, but please be careful. If Daniels left in a hurry, he might have left traps for anyone who digs too deep. I'll be around if you need backup, and please leave me with your specific plans."

"Thanks, Nathan," I said, remaining calm. "We'll be prepared for whatever he left behind. It's time we brought all of this out into the open."

Shadow and I rounded the corner near the spa. Perfect timing; I needed to clear my schedule, and find out what the Johnsons' plans were. As soon as I stepped through the door, our receptionist, Cody, grabbed my attention.

"New customer!" his voice had a lilt to it as he flashed his brilliant smile. "Both you and Lexi have new clients, actually."

Looking over his shoulder at the schedule, I saw the

notes that read: "recommendations from Tony and Rob". It was nice to see how quickly their wives booked their appointments.

"Is Lexi in?"

Cody nodded and pointed, indicating she was in her office. I stepped through the doorway and made my way through the building.

As soon as we appeared in the doorway, she looked up, waving me inside. "I'm so glad you stopped by. JJ and I are excited about this hike—really looking forward to seeing this mine you guys have told us about. But JJ is hesitant."

"He would be, wouldn't he?" I raised my brows. "I'm actually quite surprised that he's encouraged me along as much as he has with this investigation. Usually, I get the whole spiel about letting the authorities do their job." I mimicked the exact by-the-book voice he always used with me.

Lexi busted out laughing, but then a more serious tone took hold. "True. But do *you* believe we're in danger by going there?"

"I mean, *if* the mine property is part of what my father learned about ... *maybe*. I'm still not a hundred percent convinced it is. However, the insurance guy I met recently, Peter Daniels; he's up to something. I'm not entirely certain how dangerous he is, though. I mean, he's in insurance, for goodness sake."

"Well, you said he invited you and that PI to go there, right?"

I nodded. "I would like to go look around again."

"Oh? I thought you booked a tour and therefore, had a tour guide taking you inside?"

"Yeah, that's what I thought, too—that's a whole other story. But I told you about the ghost we encountered, right?

Well, that's who actually guided us."

"And that didn't freak you out? You're not afraid to go back?"

"Oddly enough—no. I'm actually quite excited." Lexi scoffed. "Then that settles it. If you're not scared, then I'm not. I'm ready to go."

"Looks like we have massages for our newfound friends' wives tomorrow morning."

"Yeah, I saw that. Tony and Rob's wives, right?"

"I actually talked to him earlier. Talk about synchronicity. He's a historian, you know. Well, I recently found out that Nathan believes the mine may have been declared a historical location as a ploy somehow related to insurance claims and the property's value. I don't understand it really, but I asked Tony if he could verify. He said he would."

"Wow, that's interesting."

"Yeah, cool he might be able to help us. And, apparently, we can help their wives."

"So, when do we leave on this expedition, then?" Lexi asked as she turned to her monitor. "I have the one appointment tomorrow morning, and I could reschedule Ms. Barker from tomorrow afternoon to whenever we get back. How long will we be gone?"

"At least two nights—so should plan for three full days."

"Ouch." Her face scrunched up as she scrolled through the schedule. "Okay, let me see what I can do."

"Yeah, I've got to figure mine out as well. Let's do that and meet back up over dinner tonight to flesh out the details with our guys?"

"Sure. You two come to ours…I've got a nice stew in the slow cooker."

"Sold. We'll be there."

CHAPTER EIGHTEEN

The aroma of Lexi's homemade stew filled the room as Greg, JJ, and I gathered around the table, maps and notes scattered between us. Joshua giggled nearby, throwing a soft toy for Shadow to fetch, while the black Lab enthusiastically trotted back and forth, her tail wagging wildly.

As we ate, Greg spread a detailed map of the Four Peaks wilderness across the table, tapping it with his finger. "So, we'll start here at the trailhead," he explained. "It's about an eight-mile hike round trip, which will take most of the day. When we did it before, we camped at the trailhead overnight and then left at daybreak."

JJ leaned in, pointing to the map. "Do we know what condition the trail is in? Last I heard, it's pretty overgrown."

I nodded. "There's been some washout from the recent rains, so we'll need to be prepared for rougher terrain. But it wasn't too bad the last time we hiked it. What was that—three or four weeks ago? Before Christmas anyway." I turned to Greg.

He agreed.

Meanwhile, Joshua squealed as Shadow dropped the toy directly onto his lap, leaning into him for an enthusiastic pat. "Go get it, Shadow!" Joshua shouted, launching the toy across the room again. Shadow dashed off, nearly clipping Greg's leg as she passed.

"Shadow will love going up there again." Greg gave the dog an approving nod. Then he grew serious again. "I'm bringing some extra gear, just in case. We don't know what Peter Daniels might've done to the site since we last checked. Last time, I sure wished I'd had protection."

I took a deep breath, glancing over at JJ. "Will you be carrying your firearm?"

He nodded. "I'd prefer not to use it, though. Do we really think …"

I cut him off before he could derail our plans. "Do we have a backup plan if we come across anything? I think as long as we plan ahead, we'll be fine. Most likely, there won't be a soul around. A living soul, at least," I chuckled.

JJ nodded, ignoring the ghostly reference. "I'll be carrying a satellite phone, just in case. We'll keep a low profile, and with the four of us, we should do fine."

"Shadow will keep us safe," Lexi chimed in. "At least we know she has rescue training."

I laughed, glancing down at Shadow, who now lay sprawled on the floor, catching her breath as Joshua draped an arm around her. She certainly didn't act like a search and rescue dog at the moment. I reached over to tousle Joshua's hair, my heart swelling with affection for the little man.

"Who's keeping Joshua?" I asked.

"He's staying with his best friend's family. They're so accommodating."

Greg started gathering up the maps. "So, I believe we all agreed we'd leave the day after tomorrow?"

We were all in agreement. That would give us a day to finish up our appointments and reschedule what we could. Then we'd have another day to pack. We agreed that Greg and I would take care of bringing the food supply. Lexi and JJ still had to inspect their gear after admitting they hadn't used it in years. They expected a run to the sporting goods store before leaving town.

As the dinner wrapped up, Lexi gathered the dishes and shot me a reassuring smile. "We've got this, Libby. We'll find out what happened to your father, one way or another."

The next day, I found myself in casual conversation with Tony's wife, Christine. The massage session began much like any other, with Christine chatting easily as I worked.

"Tony's been burning the midnight oil again," Christine said. "It's almost like he's back at his old job with all those late nights and files."

I laughed politely, though not fully understanding. "Oh, I didn't realize historians had such intense hours," I said, half-joking.

Christine gave a faint smile, as if holding back something. "Well, Tony used to be involved in … well, let's just say he had connections with a different line of work before the community college. But he's always been interested in history, so this research on the mine is kind of a blend of both worlds."

I tucked that away, unsure of what she meant. Tony's work history suddenly felt murky. Still, I didn't press, hoping a later conversation might help sort things out. Unfortunately, we never returned to that subject.

Later, Lexi filled me in on her own tabletop confessions with Rob's wife, Melissa. It sounded as though there was more to learn about these new friends. Her conversation had its own twists. As Lexi told it, halfway through their session, Melissa let something slip.

"Oh, Rob's always had a knack for sniffing out frauds and shady claims," Melissa told her with an almost fond smile. "Insurance work leaves you with many talents, I suppose."

Lexi tried to keep her tone light. "Insurance work? I thought he was in something… different?"

"Oh, he's dabbled in everything over the years," Melissa said. "But he did a lot of insurance stuff back in the day. Had a reputation for cutting through red tape—knows all the shortcuts."

Lexi told me that as she ended the session, she felt a growing suspicion. We compared notes, both finally coming to the uneasy realization: Tony and Rob were both far more connected to the insurance world than we knew.

"Isn't this too coincidental?" Lexi pushed her keyboard away, scooting her chair back, standing up, and reaching for her purse in the cabinet above her.

"Yeah. Something feels off."

"Did you mention to Christine about our hike to the mine?" she asked me, as we made our way through the building and out the front door.

"No, I said nothing, but she knew about the research he was doing for me."

"Oh, that's right, you had asked for his help."

"But Rob ... hadn't he told us he was in the investment business? Not insurance..."

"I don't know. Maybe we misunderstood."

I nodded, reaching for my keys. "Okay. Good luck shopping for new sleeping pads. We'll see you both tomorrow, bright and early."

By the time I got to my mom's house, I realized how hungry I was. She was out in her front yard watering her potted flowers. I convinced her to let me take her out to lunch and left out the part where we'd stop and do some shopping.

It wasn't long before our server at the cute café delivered our hot beverages. We placed our orders—soup and sandwich combos for both of us. I chose the grilled cheese and tomato soup; Mom opted for turkey and cheese with a cup of vegetable soup.

I watched the steam curl from my teacup as I mentally prepared my words. Mom had been so relieved to hear of the progress in her late husband's case, and I didn't want to burden her with much more, at least not yet.

"So, Mom," I began, aiming for a lighthearted tone, "Lexi, JJ, and I are planning this hiking trip soon. Just a little adventure while the weather is still so nice, you know?"

Julia looked up; her eyebrows raised with a hint of curiosity. "Oh, that sounds wonderful! Where are you heading?"

The server set down our lunch and asked if we needed anything else. We both shook our heads.

"The Four Peaks Wilderness," I replied and smiled. "It'll be a couple of days, probably three at most. JJ and Lexi want to check out the area. They were a little jealous of all our tales from the last time."

Mom chuckled. "Oh, I can imagine. So, you'll be camping, then?" She blew on her spoonful of steaming soup before gingerly trying it. "Oh, this is good."

"Yep! We'll set up camp at the trailhead the first night, then do the main hike the following morning. It'll be a long trek, but we're excited." I didn't mention the eight-mile distance or the rugged terrain, knowing my mom would only worry if she knew the full scale of the hike.

My mother's expression softened with a bit of nostalgia. "Your dad always loved taking us on hikes like that. He would have loved seeing how much you also enjoy the outdoors."

I enjoyed my grilled cheese sandwich, listening to the story she told of my first camping and fishing trip with my father.

I nodded, my heart warmed by the story. "Yeah, I thought of him, actually. And I think he would also have loved a Labrador, like Shadow, along on some of his excursions. You know, sometimes I feel he's there with me."

Julia gave a warm smile, her eyes twinkling. "I'm sure you do. The two of you were so alike. Anyway, it sounds like an amazing getaway. I'm glad you have friends like Lexi and JJ to adventure with."

We reminisced, talking about our recent travels to Alaska, and several trips I'd taken with Lexi, too. Traveling had always been deeply passionate for me. And I think I'd always known where I'd gotten it from.

Once we pushed our plates away, surrendering to our satisfied stomachs, we both declined dessert when the server came back around. She brought us our check and I insisted this meal was on me.

"So when do you leave?" Mom asked, scooting her chair back to stand up.

"We'll head out tomorrow morning," I assured her, standing up to grab my jacket.

Mom and I walked out to the car. "Oh, it sounds lovely. Enjoy it, honey. You deserve it. Just don't forget to take pictures—and let me know when you get back, all right?"

"Promise," Libby said, giving her mom a quick hug. "But I'm not dropping you quite yet. I need to pick up some food for our trip—are you up for it?"

She smiled. "I have nothing else going on. Let's go."

CHAPTER NINETEEN

The morning air was crisp, a sharp contrast to the tense excitement hanging between us. Shadow trotted by our side, sniffing the ground and occasionally looking up at us as though sensing something different in our energy. We'd spent the night camping near the trailhead, nerves preventing any proper sleep. The amethyst mine loomed somewhere ahead in the mountains, but it was clear that we all felt its pull, even from here.

As we hit the trail, the wilderness seemed to close around us. Lexi and I led the way, both focused but alert to the faint sounds and rustling in the surrounding trees.

"Are we expecting any ... unexpected visitors?" Greg muttered, glancing over his shoulder.

JJ tightened his grip on his backpack straps. "Not if

they don't know we're here. But I'm certain Daniels has people watching the place. If we're seen, there's no telling how they'll react."

Miles down the trail, we stopped for water, each of us finding a large boulder to rest up against.

"Are we close yet?" JJ asked.

Greg nodded. "Not too much farther."

As we stood again, Shadow's ears perked up, and she let out a soft whine. I crouched to pet her, whispering for her to stay close. But as I straightened, a chill swept over, and I froze, spotting something on the trail ahead—a vague figure in old, dusty clothes.

The ghostly miner's form was transparent, his outline shifting in the sunlight filtering through the trees. I felt goosebumps as he raised a hand, pointing up the trail.

"Turn back," the miner's voice echoed in my mind, quiet but insistent. "Danger lies ahead."

Lexi gasped, gripping my arm, but JJ, ever practical, whispered, "Is that the miner you told us about?"

I nodded, glancing between the old miner and my friends. "He's ... uh, warning us."

Shadow growled low, her eyes stared straight ahead into the trees, and her stance protective. But the miner's form flickered, his warning hanging in the air. Just as he vanished, we heard a faint snap of a branch behind us.

Turning, we saw another figure in the distance, dressed in dark clothing, quickly blending back into the trees. JJ pulled out his phone and shook his head in frustration, as there was no signal. "Looks like we're not alone," he muttered. "Think it could be Daniels or even Ross? We'd better keep moving."

"It could be other hikers," Greg added. "The mining

company doesn't own all this land. In fact, most of it is national forest, but we're getting close now."

We continued, but every now and then, I swore I saw the shadowy figure again, slipping through the trees as if tracking our progress. When we reached a narrow pass, Lexi stopped, whispered, "Guys, look."

Ahead, two men stood, blocking the trail. "You all should turn back," one hollered, his tone leaving no room for debate. "This isn't a place you want to be."

I stepped forward anyway. "Uh, could you tell us where does this trail lead? We thought we were following our hiking guide." I pointed, indicating it was in my pack.

The other man's eyes flickered, but he kept a solid stance. "Ma'am, this is private property. For your own safety, you'll need to head back that way." He used his hand in a circular manner, motioning for us to turn around.

A tense silence ensued as we glanced around at each other. JJ finally spoke. "No problem, man. We must have taken a wrong turn somewhere."

I started to protest, when Greg gently took my arm, bringing my attention to his GPS device. Pointing to the display, he whispered between clinched teeth, "Not now, Libby. Let's go. We'll find another way."

The first muscled man muttered something under his breath, exchanging a final, loaded look with his buddy. We simply turned away and headed down the trail.

Shadow growled, her fur standing up, and her eyes kept darting with glances behind us. Each of us remained quiet, deep in thought, as we considered our next steps.

We pushed forward along the narrow mountain path. Shadow remained alert, occasionally casting another peek behind, her hackles raised as if she could sense more than what we could see. I thought of my father, and the reason we came here. I sure hoped we could figure out a way to get past their security.

In nature's quiet solitude, there was no mistaking when the sound of the rotors reached our ears.

"Over here!" JJ hollered, grabbing my arm and pulling me into a copse of trees. Shadow, Lexi, and Greg followed. We all crouched to the ground.

South of us, we heard the loud, whirring sounds of a helicopter. It sped off over the horizon as suddenly as it'd appeared. Quietness settled over before we stood again.

Checking the skies, Greg murmured. "Think they're looking for us?"

JJ shook his head. "Nah. Not at that speed. If they were looking for us, they'd be slowly making circles wherever the trails go. I think they left."

Shadow's head turned to face the path we'd stepped away from. She tugged at the leash, wanting to get moving.

I held on to the leash tight, also staring down the trail. "So, what are you guys thinking? Should we try the mine again?"

"Maybe we should wait until dark?" Lexi suggested.

Greg nodded. "I agree. We're not sure who left on that helicopter. The guards could still be there for sure."

I definitely didn't want to wait until dark. "What if we quietly start that way and do some reconnaissance first? If they have left, we'll continue on. Let's just see what we're dealing with first."

We all agreed, and started that direction. When we got about an eighth of a mile from where we'd last seen those bulky men, we carefully maneuvered through the trees and brush.

JJ halted, so we all did. "I don't see anyone, do you?"

I took out my binoculars and carefully scanned the area. "All quiet."

JJ motioned for us to continue. We proceeded slowly, every step cautiously placed. Even Shadow seemed to understand the protocol.

As we neared the mine's entrance, I abruptly stopped. An unease settled in my stomach seconds before the ghostly miner appeared. His figure was almost solid now, as though he drew strength from the mine.

"Proceed with caution," he muttered. "What's hidden was meant to stay buried."

"Why?" I whispered aloud, my voice barely more than a breath. "Who's here besides you?"

The miner's expression was neutral as he shook his head. "It's okay. I'll guide you. Come." He pointed to the entrance, slowly stepping over the threshold. Then he vanished into the ether like mist.

Lexi and I exchanged nervous glances. JJ and Greg, each giving it careful consideration. We were so close.

CHAPTER TWENTY

Deep inside the mine, after navigating the first few familiar, narrow tunnels, we saw our ghost friend ahead of us. We followed him.

Lexi whispered, "Are you sure this is safe?"

"We've been this far before," I assured her.

"No, what about *him*." She pointed to the apparition we followed.

"We're fine."

Shadow let out a soft woof.

Lexi muttered skeptically, "Uh, huh."

I turned to the guys, who were only steps behind us. "We should be getting close, right?"

Greg nodded.

Footsteps crunched ahead of us. We came to an abrupt

halt. I pointed my flashlight straight ahead, scanning both left and right. Our ghostly guide disappeared. Emerging from the shadows came Detective Ross and Peter Daniels. Ross's fierce glare gave us pause. Daniels had the faintest smirk, as though he'd been waiting for us to walk into his trap all along.

"We had a feeling you'd show up," Ross said, his tone icy. "You know, this is no place for hikers."

Daniels moved closer, his eyes zeroing in on me. "Curiosity runs deep in your family, doesn't it?" he sneered. "But I'll say it again: some things are better left alone, Libby."

Greg moved protectively beside me, meeting Daniels's gaze with defiance. "Libby deserves to know the truth about her father. Whatever's hidden here, we're not leaving until we have answers."

Daniels chuckled darkly, exchanging a look with Ross. "I think you'll find your journey ends here. This mine is private property, and I'm not afraid to call for enforcement, if needed."

JJ cleared his throat, bravely stepping forward. "And I think you'll find you're on thin ice here, Daniels. Whatever you're hiding won't stay hidden much longer."

Suddenly, another man appeared from the shadows, taking a position at Daniel's side. Rob—one of the two we met previously at the sushi restaurant—stood there, his stare unrelenting. Lexi and I looked at each other, stunned, and realizing now that our sushi bar meeting was anything but coincidence. Was he in on this with the rest of them?

Daniels stepped closer to me, his voice dropping low. "You think you're clever, piecing things together. But do you really know what your father got himself involved in? The truth could destroy you."

Through the tension, Shadow gave a low, protective growl, standing close to me. The ghostly miner reappeared, his figure hovering nearby, although no one else seemed to react to his presence. I saw his face fill with grief as he watched our exchange with the powerful men.

I looked at my friends, then at Daniels. "We're here now. You might as well give us that tour you reneged on. How about it, Peter?"

"This is as far as we go. Now, let's turn around and we'll see you out."

"We're not leaving until we have answers," I boldly stated, even while quaking inside. "C'mon, show us the way. If you have nothing to hide, it shouldn't be a problem, right?"

Daniels and Ross squinted, confused. Finally, Daniels used his hands, signaling a clear path ahead. "Fine. Go ahead."

JJ and Greg hesitated. I guided Shadow around the three intimidating men, and slowly Greg, JJ, and Lexi were on our heels. With another peek behind me, I shouted, "We're waiting, Daniels! Show us the way."

I saw Alan Ross become agitated. He grumbled at his comrade, "What are you doing, Pete? They're getting away!"

"Let them go. They'll never find their way out of there. They're as good as dead."

One more look back before they were out of our sight, and I saw them retreat. We continued on.

Replaying the miner's warnings and Daniels and Ross's threats, I was shocked that the men hadn't followed. We kept moving, regardless. Shadow stuck close by my side, her ears perked and her nose occasionally dipping to the ground, catching scents.

We reached the familiar area where the mine expanded into a wide chamber. The walls glittered faintly with violet hues—the amethyst veins we'd seen before. I paused, running my hand over the rough rock, feeling a connection. *Had my father once stood here, looking at these very stones?*

We proceeded, leading Lexi and JJ to the next chamber where we'd previously found the hidden room. Our friendly ghost appeared again, reminding us which turn in the tunnel system to take. As we made our way into the next cavern, the strong iron door we'd opened previously remained open. *Had no one been down this far since our last visit?*

Greg cast his flashlight beam throughout the vast room. JJ and Lexi admired in awe, noticing all the artifacts and scrolls scattered about. Then, in the far corner, he caught sight of an old wooden box half-buried in the dirt. Greg led us across the room. "Libby, come look at this. We missed this before."

I knelt beside him, carefully brushing away dust and dirt to reveal it. The box was heavy and locked, with a faint insignia on its lid that looked suspiciously familiar.

Lexi gasped softly. "Libby, isn't that the same symbol you showed us from your father's files?"

I nodded, my pulse quickening. "Yes. I think this might have been his…" I searched my backpack for a small multitool, then carefully worked to pry open the lock. The box gave a soft click, and with a trembling hand, I opened it.

Weathered documents, faded photos, and a small notebook scrawled with my father's handwriting were inside. I lifted it carefully, flipping through the pages. The entries described his investigations, his suspicions about a fraudulent scheme involving the mine, and cryptic references to Daniels, Ross, and many others in the insurance company.

"His handwriting," I whispered. "More notes that could help our case."

JJ examined the documents over my shoulder. His brow furrowed. "It looks like he found evidence that the mine was being used to launder money and hide certain ... *disposal operations*," he said, pausing as he processed the implications.

"Disposal?" Greg asked. "You mean—"

But before he could finish, the sound of footsteps echoed through the tunnel. Our flashlights swung in unison, where shadows moved ominously. Daniels, Ross, and Rob appeared; their faces meant business this time.

"Found something interesting, did you? Our hiding spot, I see," Daniels sneered, his eyes glinting with satisfaction as he took in our discoveries. "I told you— curiosity would get you into trouble, Ms. Madsen," he playfully taunted in a sing-songy voice.

Detective Ross stepped forward, gun in hand, his expression colder than ever. "Your tour is over. Whatever you think you've found here, you won't be walking out with it."

Terrified, I looked at my friends, realizing that our only way out was forward, deeper into the mine. A quick exchange of horrified glances confirmed we'd all come to that conclusion.

CHAPTER TWENTY-ONE

I took a step back, trying to keep my tone calm. "This mine, this whole operation—there are already enough records here to expose you," I said, trying to keep my nerves in check. "You think you can hide everything away in here and no one can touch you? Well, you can't hide forever."

Daniels chuckled, a hollow sound that echoed in the chamber. "The people we work with? They can make anything disappear. What makes you think you're any different?"

As the men advanced, Shadow growled a deep, throaty rumble. In a flash of inspiration, I held up my flashlight, casting it directly into Daniels's eyes, causing him to stumble back in temporary blindness. My friends followed suit, beaming their ultrabright lights into the other two men's eyes.

Shadow charged one of their dark figures and we heard the man scream.

Seizing the moment, I grabbed the box of evidence and we sprinted.

A gunshot sounded, sending a shrill echo through the cavernous space. Another scream resonated, and we ran for our lives.

Our footfalls reverberated as we dashed through the tunnel system. Light from our flashlights ping-ponging off the walls around us as we sprinted. I felt Shadow tear by me. Greg's voice sounded, pressing me to go faster. I risked a quick glance behind me and made out Lexi's silhouette running.

"JJ!" I screamed.

"Just run, Libby!"

The tunnel twisted and turned, the path narrowing again. We could hear shouts and another gunshot from far behind us, but a flickering light ahead signaled that we were reaching another opening.

Finally, we burst into a smaller, hidden chamber. My breath caught—*Oh no, we'll get trapped going that way.*

Just then, our ghost guide appeared and pointed to the new tunnel.

I looked at him, confused. "Won't we get stuck?"

"*Escape...*" he breathed, with no actual sound produced.

"Over there!" Lexi whispered, pointing ahead. As we raced toward it, the apparition appeared again in the shadows—his translucent form gesturing to keep going.

"Is that some kind of shaft?" Greg shouted.

JJ saw it and said, "Run!"

I looked at our miner friend with the question in my eyes.

"Go. The truth will find its way out, but you must live to tell it," he whispered; his form wavering. "I'll take care of them."

I took one last look, my heart filled with gratitude, and then we scrambled into the escape shaft. Behind us, the sound of angry voices and footsteps grew loud as Daniels and his men closed in on us. But the miner stopped them, and my friends and I made our way toward the surface.

As we crawled through the narrow opening, a dim glow ahead guided us like a beacon. We were bruised, tired, and tense, but we pressed on. Finally, after what felt like an eternity, we reached the surface, emerging into the night air.

I gulped in the fresh air, grateful for the open sky above. Shadow panted heavily and I grabbed for her leash.

Greg checked the area, his eyes scanning for any signs of Daniels, Ross, or their men. "Looks like we lost them, but we shouldn't hang around." He pulled out his GPS and pointed to his left. "That way—hurry, let's get back to the trailhead."

As we made our way down the rugged mountain path, JJ pulled out his phone and checked for a signal. After a few moments, he looked up, nodding. "I'll call it in. Daniels and Ross have connections, but they're on the wrong side of the law. I have enough on them to get internal affairs involved, and now, with what we found, they'll have to answer some serious questions."

For hours, as we navigated the terrain through the darkness, I felt confident knowing that the box was secure in my backpack. With my father's notebook, the worn pages being a tangible reminder of the man he was and the risks he'd taken to protect our family, nothing would stop me from getting these guys behind bars.

I turned to Lexi with my thoughts. "He tried so hard to do the right thing, even when it meant he was alone in an investigation."

As we trekked, following the winding path, and emerging from desert overgrowth, we stopped in our tracks. Headlights appeared in the distance.

CHAPTER TWENTY-TWO

We all lunged behind the tall scrub brush, huddled together, hoping not to be discovered.

"How did they make it down so quickly?" I whispered.

JJ only put his finger over his lips, shushing me.

Greg quietly peeked out. The lights from the vehicle had turned off. A man slid out from the driver's seat and walked to the front of his SUV. His eyes scanned the area and then he turned to get back in the car.

I tried to stop Greg, but he stood before I reached his pant legs. "What are you doing?" I hissed.

"Guys, it's okay." He turned and waved for the rest of us to follow him.

JJ nodded. "I texted him when I found a signal. Glad he got it."

After my eyes adjusted, I finally saw it actually was Nathan. Relief swept over me and I could also see now that we were close to the trailhead.

Nathan's expression varied from worry to relief as he saw us approach.

"Are you all okay?" Nathan asked, concern lacing his voice.

"We're okay, thanks to each other and…" I paused, thinking of the ghostly miner. I didn't say more, but the others knew who I meant. "We found more than we bargained for. Daniels and Ross are behind everything. They've been covering up their activities, laundering money and … *worse.*"

Nathan nodded, a spark of understanding in his eyes. "Then we'll take this to the right people. We will not let them cover it up again."

We regrouped at the trailhead, exhausted. Nathan made calls to some trusted contacts in law enforcement, those he knew would hear us out without interference.

Greg put his arm around me, pulling me in tightly as I leaned into him, comforted by his presence. "What's next, Libby? Do you want to go public with this?"

I considered it, clutching my bag which contained all the evidence. "Yes. People need to know the truth, not just for him, but for everyone hurt by these men." I looked at my friends, who all nodded their agreement.

As dawn approached, our group prepared to return home, carrying not only new evidence but also a sense of closure for my father and everyone impacted by Daniels and Ross's corruption. Greg, Shadow, and I piled into Nathan's SUV, while JJ and Lexi agreed to get my 4Runner back to town. We'd pick it up later.

As we arrived back in town, Nathan suggested we meet with the trusted detective he'd called earlier. Someone outside of Daniels and Ross's influence, he promised. We headed straight for a small coffee shop downtown, where Detective Renee Alvarez was waiting. We were told she was a no-nonsense investigator with a reputation for rooting out corruption, and her intense, fixed stare told me she meant business.

Clutching my father's notebook tightly, I shared everything: my father's suspicions, the hidden mine records, and the shocking role Daniels and Ross played in covering up crimes tied to the mine. Detective Alvarez listened carefully, her face becoming more serious with each detail. She flipped through the pages I handed her.

"Libby, what you and your friends found is explosive," Detective Alvarez said finally. "This notebook alone may have enough to push for a warrant. In the meantime, gather the rest of the information you have from home and get it over to me. Daniels and Ross won't know what hit them."

She vowed to act quickly, but given the stakes, she suggested we keep a low profile for now.

Greg and I agreed, then called JJ to pick us up. Despite feeling exhausted, we were hopeful. Even so, my thoughts ran wild, trying to sort through everything. As JJ drove us across town, I felt an uneasy feeling, one of unfinished business. That's when it came to me. There was one more person I needed answers from—Tony, the so-called 'historian'. I needed to know how he and his friend, Rob, figured into all of this.

First, I needed some sleep after an awfully long night. Then, I would find my answers.

Later that evening, I called Tony. My voice was firm; I

was done with the half-truths. Rob accompanying Daniels and Ross on the mining property had really thrown me off course.

"Tony, I know you're not who you said you were," I stated directly. "If you don't want the cops looking into your past, you'd better start being honest with me about what's really going on with that mine."

There was a long silence on the other end of the line. Then Tony sighed, his voice resigned. "Fine, Libby. Meet me tomorrow. But you won't like what you hear."

CHAPTER TWENTY-THREE

The next day, Shadow and I met Tony at a quiet park, with JJ nearby for backup. From the moment he arrived, Tony seemed almost defeated, as though carrying the truth had worn him down. He revealed the full extent of the cover-up: Peter Daniels and his cronies in the insurance company had been hiding financial misconduct for years, leveraging the mine as a dumping ground and cash cow for illicit operations.

And Tony had been involved too, though at the time, he hadn't known just how dark things would get. By the time he learned, it was too late; he was tangled up with them and couldn't find a way out.

"But Libby," Tony said, his voice breaking slightly, "I didn't know it was your dad they'd … uh, silenced. They told me he'd died of a heart attack."

"So, you *did know* who I was that night at the bar, then? You and Rob stalked me, found *me*."

He looked confused.

"Oh, come on, Tony. We first met at a sushi bar … you knew exactly who I was. Who sent you there?"

His eyes widened and his hands flew up. "That was actually coincidental that we ran into you and Lexi that night. It wasn't until you exchanged business cards with me that I recognized the Madsen name. Honestly." He hung his head, then slowly his eyes met mine again. "I've never been able to forgive myself for my involvement, after I learned about Leon's passing. Once I figured out you were his daughter—I felt even worse. You and Lexi were so kind to us—our wives appreciated the massages. But *none of it* had to do with the business I got caught up in with the insurance company."

Hearing this confirmation hurt, but it also fueled me to continue.

"Then help me, Tony," I said. "You owe me that much. Tell Alvarez everything you know."

With Tony's confession, I felt we might finally have what we needed to ensure Daniels, Ross, and anyone else involved would face the consequences. With Nathan's help and Detective Alvarez's commitment to justice, I finally felt we were making progress.

* * *

Later that afternoon, and sitting at my mother's kitchen table, my thoughts ran wildly as I waited for her and Jordan to take their seats. In her typical fashion, Mom set down a tray of coffee mugs and some sweet treats. Jordan poured herself a cup, glancing at me with anticipation.

I took a deep breath. "Mom, Jordan, I know we've all had questions about Dad's death. Questions that have recently haunted us, honestly. And I've finally found some answers—ones that ... well, they may be hard to accept."

My mom's hands stilled, and Jordan gave me a sharp look. "What are you talking about, Libby?"

I opened my father's notebook, flipping to a page of notes in his precise handwriting.

"We were right. There was more to Dad's heart attack than natural causes. His job, as an insurance adjuster, put him in danger. He uncovered fraud in the insurance company. More specifically, the people he was about to expose made sure he wouldn't divulge anything."

My mother's hand went to her mouth, her face paling. "Are you suggesting that someone deliberately hurt him?"

I nodded, my voice tightening. "Yes, that is what I believe, Mom. Dad had uncovered information linking some dangerous people to insurance fraud and illegal activities. We discovered, oddly enough, that much of it tied to the mine Greg and I stumbled across. Peter Daniels and Detective Ross, along with others in the company, have gone to extreme lengths to cover up their crimes. And Dad, well ... he was in their way. We're still trying to figure out the specifics—*who* specifically killed him. *How...* there are still many unanswered questions."

Mom's expression shifted. "He never said anything. I knew he was under stress, but he was always so careful about what he shared about work. I thought ... I thought his work was safe."

Jordan set her cup down, staring at Libby with disbelief.

"But how did you find this out? You've figured all this out on your own?"

"Not alone," I assured her. "I've had help—from Greg, JJ, Lexi, and even Nathan Pierce. Apparently, he'd worked with Dad before ... well, before he died. And just recently, I got confirmation from another man who was involved. Dad was onto something big, and he didn't back down, even though it was risky."

Mom shook her head, tears forming. "Your father was the most honest man I knew. He never would've compromised what he believed in. But I can't believe this, that he was actually taken from us over a corrupt insurance claim! That makes me angry."

I reached out, taking my mother's hand. "Mom, he was trying to protect people. He was uncovering secrets and trying to do good."

Jordan leaned in, her voice shaky. "What are we going to do about it, Libby? We can't let them get away with this."

"Detective Alvarez, someone we trust, is already on the case. And we've given her everything we've found. With Dad's notebooks and other evidence we've collected, we have a real chance at solving this."

Mom clasped my hand tightly, a glimmer of pride through the tears. "Your father would be so proud of you, Libby. And I am, too. I don't know how you did it, how you found the strength."

I smiled, feeling my eyes well up. "I think I got it from him, actually—and from you both. He fought for us, and now we can fight for him."

CHAPTER TWENTY-FOUR

Before heading home, I tried Detective Alvarez's number, hoping it would be a good time to drop off the boxes of evidence I'd promised her. After a few rings, it went to voice mail and I left a message for her to return my call. As soon as I punched the button to end the call, I saw Nathan Pierce's name pop up on my display.

"Hi Nathan," I answered.

"Libby, have you handed over the documents to Renee?"

"I just left a message for her—she didn't answer."

"Okay. Well, I have a meeting already scheduled for late afternoon. I could take them myself, if you'd like?"

"Oh. Shouldn't I be joining you, then?" I asked, curious why I knew nothing of this meeting.

He cleared his throat. "No, no. The meeting is about some other business we're working on together." After a slight pause, and another cough, he added, "I only thought I could save you a trip to her office."

Feeling slightly embarrassed for thinking that my case was the only one he could possibly be working on, I agreed, gave him my address, and then hung up.

An unease settled over me, wondering if I should have planned to make copies of everything before handing it off. Too late now, but it made me wish I had done that instead of stopping over at Mom's earlier.

Greg's truck was in the driveway when I pulled up. I hustled inside and hurriedly glanced through the boxes, regretting my decision to hand everything over now. I pulled several documents from their files and snapped photos of them. Hurriedly, I tore through files, trying to remember the most important pieces of evidence I'd seen.

"Oh, you're home," Greg and Shadow came in from the backyard and stopped cold in their tracks. "What's wrong? What are you doing?" He gave me a side-eye, watching me hurtle files aside and take the next picture.

"Nothing really. Nathan is on his way over to grab these boxes and he'll take them to Detective Alvarez."

"You're letting the precious cargo out of your custody?" he gently teased.

"I don't think I have a choice—it's evidence. Help me."

He stepped over and collected the files I'd already been through. "Ok. What are you upset about then, Libs?"

"Oh, I guess I am feeling like they're pushing me out now … like I'll no longer be part of the investigation. Isn't that silly?"

The doorbell sounded and Shadow ran, barking.

"Oh shit. I wanted to get those last two files. Here," I handed him my phone. "Get as many pages in that file as you can."

Without question, he did as he was told.

I grabbed the dog's collar. "C'mon, Shadow. Get back." I opened the door a crack. She began barking ferociously when she saw the man standing there. "Greg, can you … after… ?" Greg understood and kept snapping pictures.

"Sorry, Nathan. She rarely gets so worked up." I apologized, stepping outside to greet him on the front porch. "Greg will get her settled and then I'll get you those boxes."

After an uncomfortable minute or two, Greg opened the front door, ushering us inside to the kitchen table. "Sorry about that. She's a little triggered today apparently," he explained, with a forced grin.

Greg gave another command to Shadow, who still hadn't settled down. Reluctantly, she stopped barking, but as Nathan moved closer to the boxes, her growl intensified.

"Wow, there are a lot of boxes, aren't there?" he mentioned, as he cast a nervous glance in Shadow's direction.

"Yeah, we'll help you load them up," I said, lifting the one closest to me. Greg followed suit and grabbed another as we all walked out to his car. "So, you work regularly with Alvarez, then?"

He nodded. "Known her for years."

Nathan quickly left after we had everything loaded, saying he was already late. Walking back inside, Greg and I let out a sigh of relief. I picked up my phone from the kitchen table and scrolled through the photos, seeing what we got.

Greg noted Nathan seemed stressed. I hadn't specifically noticed that, but Shadow sure got agitated, so maybe that was why. She had picked up on his anxiety.

Distractedly scrolling, I mentioned, "I'm going to give Detective Alvarez a call in the morning and see if I can meet with her. Just need to be sure they don't push me out now."

Greg nodded. "Might not be a bad idea. Want me to go with you?"

"Nah. You have work. I'll do this myself."

* * *

It took several days to reach Alvarez. I walked up the steps to her precinct, noting it was a precinct across town I hadn't known existed. I'd only ever been to where JJ worked.

I was greeted by a nice gentleman at the front desk, where I asked to speak to Detective Alvarez. Sitting in the hard, plastic chairs in the lobby, I watched people busily go about their work. Half an hour later, Renee came and ushered me down a long hallway. Stepping into her office, I immediately eyed the boxes Nathan had recently brought to her. The cluttered desk and stacks of files seemed to consume the dim, narrow space. Renee greeted me with a warm smile and gestured toward a chair, but I sensed a hint of impatience in the detective's movements. I brushed it off—Renee was busy, after all, and had agreed to help despite being swamped.

"Alright, let's see what we've got here." Renee leaned

forward as I pulled out the first file from a box marked "Coronado Fire—Personal."

"These are mostly my father's notes from his cases," I explained, flipping open a page filled with his familiar handwriting. I felt a pang of longing as I scanned his words, the same notes he'd scribbled just before his unexpected death. "He was meticulous, but here... I think he was on to something. See these notes about 'irregularities in structural assessments'?"

Renee's expression didn't shift, but her eyes narrowed slightly as she scanned the pages. "Huh," she murmured, her voice neutral. "Looks like he went beyond his duties as an adjuster." She leaned back and tapped the page thoughtfully, but her eyes quickly flitted to the stack of files I hadn't yet opened. "He wrote all this down?"

I nodded. "He took his work seriously. If something seemed off, he kept track of it."

Renee's mouth pulled into a tight line. "Or maybe he just got in over his head," she said, the words flat.

I frowned slightly, taken aback by the remark, but shook it off.

I opened the next box, which contained a black leather ledger buried beneath various files. "This wasn't something he would normally keep. My dad wasn't one for ledgers," I remarked, opening it up. Shorthand notes, initials, and rows of dollar amounts covered the pages.

Renee stiffened, her gaze sharpened as she took the ledger from me. She examined a few pages closely, her brow furrowing. "These entries look like some sort of personal documentation. See here, 'Property damage, $250K: H&W Amethyst Group' and another one, 'Fire loss, $300K: Kline Holdings.' Those aren't typical for a claims adjuster to keep track of."

My stomach twisted as I recognized some names from my earlier research. "Those are tied to claims around the Coronado Fire," I said slowly, feeling a chill. "I think he was tracking something bigger, maybe he thought these payments were connected somehow."

Renee nodded, but her reaction seemed restrained. What was she holding back? "Possibly, or he could've made a mistake," she said, her tone suddenly dismissive. "Let's not jump to conclusions."

I blinked, taken aback. "It's not like my dad to make mistakes, especially not with something this detailed. He was thorough."

Renee pressed her lips together, forcing a smile that didn't reach her eyes. "Sure, but this is only speculation at this point. Let's keep going." Her hand rested on the ledger a moment too long before she placed it down and moved on.

In the next box, I pulled out a stack of photos. My father appeared in several of them, standing before the entrance of what looked like a large, dark mineshaft. I recognized the jagged rocks and dusty landscape—it had to be the same amethyst mine.

Renee stiffened. "This doesn't look like a casual inspection. Who's this man next to him?" she asked, pointing to a tall figure standing with my father.

My heart skipped. "That's ... that's Peter Daniels. He works at the insurance agency."

"Interesting," Renee replied, a flicker of something unreadable crossing her face before she composed herself. "Maybe Daniels reached out to him for his expertise." But her voice held a slight edge, as if she knew more than she let on. "I'll do some digging on Daniels to see if there's anything else. But, Libby," she paused, looking directly at me, "be careful about getting your hopes up. These things are never as clear-cut as they seem."

I met her gaze, the odd tone in her voice giving me pause. "I know, but I need answers."

Renee smiled again, her expression softening. "I understand. Let's just keep it between us for now, alright?"

I nodded, grateful to have Renee's support. But as I packed up, doubts lingered. *If my father hadn't figured it out, what made me think I could?*

* * *

Renee watched her go, her warm smile fading the moment the door closed. She swiftly pulled the blinds down to ensure privacy. Then she hastily navigated around the desk to take her seat, picking up the ledger again and flipped to the pages showing the entries about the mine.

Her eyes skimmed over each line with a keen intensity, absorbing every detail. Renee's expression darkened as she reached a particular page that listed several payments that hadn't been mentioned in any public records. She saw that each payment connected to small companies and shell corporations.

Closing the ledger, she tapped her long ruby-red fingernails on the desk, contemplating her next move. The stakes had risen with Libby Madsen's increasing involvement, and she could tell that Ms. Madsen would not butt out anytime soon. Libby's determination was unsettling, connecting dots that could expose the entire network.

Picking up her phone, she dialed a number she rarely used.

"We may have a problem," Renee murmured into the receiver when the deep voice on the other end picked up. "Libby Madsen found her father's ledger. She's getting close, figuring things out, and they've got the *old* files, records that could lead them directly to us."

A pause. The voice on the line responded with a tone Renee knew all too well: cold, calculating, and completely unyielding.

"I understand," Renee replied, nodding as she listened to the instructions. "I'll make sure it doesn't come to that. But if she keeps poking around, she's going to become a risk we can't ignore."

After hanging up, Renee took a deep breath. She understood her responsibilities, and despite her reluctance, she knew she couldn't back down. She glanced down at the ledger again and made a mental note of the specific files she would need to alter to keep Libby and her friends off track. For now, it was all about playing it cool and giving Libby just enough information to feel like she was making progress—while ensuring that the trail went cold before it led anywhere dangerous.

With a final glance at the ledger, she locked it away in her private drawer.

CHAPTER TWENTY-FIVE

The next morning, I called Detective Alvarez's office, eager to continue combing through my father's file boxes. I'd hardly slept, my head swirling with all the clues we'd uncovered the day before. Each piece brought us closer to answers, but they still felt disjointed, like a puzzle missing the key parts to putting away Peter Daniels and Alan Ross for life.

"Detective Alvarez's office," Renee answered, her tone calm and professional, yet friendly enough that I felt instantly at ease.

"Detective, it's Libby. I was wondering if you had time today to go over more of my dad's notes together? I can bring coffee, maybe?"

Renee's warm laugh echoed through the phone.

"Coffee sounds good," she replied smoothly. "I'm free after eleven, if that works for you. And feel free to bring any other items, if you have something. I'll make sure we have a couple of hours uninterrupted."

"That'd be great, thanks. I have a few things from his desk I'd like to bring over," I said, a spark of hope kindling in my chest. "Oh, and can I bring my dog?"

"Uh, no. No dogs allowed in the office."

"No problem." I glanced down at Shadow, who already seemed to understand she was getting left behind again.

"Perfect. I'll see you soon." Her avid voice was friendly, and free of the guardedness I'd sometimes felt from others when I brought up my father's investigation. There was no hint of the tension Renee exuded the day before, only her usual patience and professionalism.

At eleven on the dot, I arrived at her office, balancing two cups of coffee in one hand and clutching a small box of personal items in the other. Renee greeted me at the door, with her perfectly coifed dark hair and immaculate business attire, and her usual composed demeanor as reassuring as always.

"Thank you for the coffee, Libby." She gestured for me to sit as she took a sip, nodding approvingly. "Let's see what we've got."

I smiled, pulling a few items from the box, including a small journal I'd found in my mother's attic. "I thought this might have some details about the people he was working with on the Coronado fire," I explained, flipping through the pages. "He usually kept records of his client interactions, but this was … well, it's a little different."

Renee's eyes scanned the open journal with interest, but her expression didn't falter. She leaned in, giving an encouraging nod to a few entries that listed names tied to companies she suspected being related to the mine. She asked careful questions, guiding me down paths that felt promising but ultimately led nowhere.

"These notes are helpful," Renee said, her voice full of encouragement. "It's possible these companies he listed here may have connections we haven't uncovered yet. Do you have other names or companies you might want us to investigate?"

I chewed my lip, thinking. "None other than Kline Holdings and H&W Amethyst Group, which we discovered yesterday—do you think this helps us nail Peter Daniels and Alan Ross?"

Renee nodded, glancing down at her own notebook. "It's possible, but we still have to tie them directly to those holding companies. We're getting closer—I feel it. Your father must've had a sense something was wrong, and he wasn't willing to back down. It's impressive." She offered a small, sympathetic smile. "Not everyone in the field goes that extra mile."

I looked down, admiring her manicure. "If he felt it was worth the extra effort, then it's worth it for us to keep going."

Renee's face softened. "We'll keep digging, and if anything suspicious comes up, you'll be the first to know. This is important, Libby."

A wave of gratitude surged through me.

As we wrapped up, Renee guided the conversation in a new direction. "One thing to consider, Libby, is taking a break every so often. You don't want to burn yourself out, especially with how personal this all is. It might help to take some of the pressure off, just a bit."

I nodded, not fully convinced but touched by her concern. "I appreciate that. Maybe once we make a little more headway."

Renee's smile was gentle as she showed me out. "Absolutely. And remember, you have support."

* * *

Watching her go, Renee's expression darkened. She'd kept Libby in the dark—at least for now. But with each new clue, Libby was inching closer to truths that Renee wasn't sure she could keep hidden for long.

As the door closed behind Libby, Renee leaned back in her chair, her fingers tapping thoughtfully on the armrest. Each visit from Libby was becoming riskier; every piece of evidence that woman uncovered threatened to unravel the carefully constructed narrative Renee and her network had spent years building. She'd managed to keep Libby off course for now, but she could feel the noose tightening with each discovery.

Renee ran her hand across the smooth leather of the notebook, considering her next move. Peter Daniels was supposed to be handling this situation from the shadows, but his recent shenanigans had thrown everything off-balance. What was he thinking, agreeing to meet with Libby Madsen? Much less offering to take her for a mine tour? Was he mad?

Now, she had the responsibility to handle Libby directly, fully aware that if Libby persisted at this pace, it would only be a matter of time before she uncovered information Renee couldn't control. And with the trail leading to the mine, even the slightest misstep could expose their entire operation.

"She's tenacious," Renee muttered under her breath, a flicker of something like admiration passing through her mind before she pushed it away. The risk outweighed any respect she might have for Libby's perseverance. It must run in the Madsen's blood. Libby's father had been just as persistent—and look where that had led him. If history was anything to go by, Libby would follow the same path. Unless someone stopped her soon.

But eliminating her wasn't a straightforward option. Libby's connections to Detective Jeff Johnson and others in the department complicated matters. Too much interference could draw unwanted attention, and she needed to be subtle, undetectable, and, ideally, keep Libby close—feeding her just enough information to make her believe progress was being made, while obscuring the genuine threats she was about to uncover.

Renee's thoughts shifted to Rob Turner, her investment banker and reluctant ally in this scheme. He'd been useful, if not entirely reliable. The fact Libby knew of him now wasn't ideal, but there was still time to cover those tracks. It was up to Renee to cover their involvement with the money laundering, insurance fraud, and the disposal site. And if Libby ever got her hands on those records, there'd be no salvaging Rob's record—or her own.

"I need to find a new diversion," Renee murmured, glancing at her desk phone. She had a few ideas—people who could subtly mislead Libby further or sow seeds of doubt in her current leads. But if Libby continued down this path, a stronger response would be necessary. A flicker of regret surfaced, but Renee quickly dismissed it. She couldn't afford weakness now.

CHAPTER TWENTY-SIX

Greg entered the jewelry shop with a sense of anticipation buzzing through him. The same bell chimed overhead, and he noticed the jeweler glancing up from his workbench. Recognizing Greg, the older man stood, a warm smile crossing his face as he retrieved a small velvet box from behind the counter.

"Ah, Mr. Lawson," he greeted in a warm tone. "I think you're going to love the result."

Greg approached the counter, barely able to contain his excitement. The gentleman placed the box gently in front of him, lifting the lid to reveal the custom-designed ring. Greg's breath caught. The craftsmanship was undeniable. The jeweler had flawlessly set the amethysts on either side of the princess-cut diamond, and it shimmered in a way that somehow felt more meaningful than any ring he'd ever seen. Diamonds and amethysts together now, they sparkled with a warmth that brought back every memory of the hike, the mine, and the spirit they'd left behind.

"It's beautiful," Greg said, his voice barely above a whisper as he took in the fine detailing. "You really brought it to life."

The jeweler nodded, clearly pleased with his work. "I wanted it to feel timeless and unique, just like the story you told me. Those amethysts hold history—and now, they're part of your future."

Greg slid the box into his pocket carefully. He could almost picture Libby's face when he gave it to her, knowing she'd understand the significance of every facet, every piece of history that had led them to the present moment.

"Thank you," he said, his voice filled with gratitude.

"It's my pleasure, Mr. Lawson. I hope it brings you both all the luck and happiness in the world."

Greg left the store with the ring securely in his pocket, ready to make his proposal even more special than he'd originally planned.

Yet, as he left the jewelers with the ring nestled safely in his pocket, a subtle unease settled over him. His memory kept flickering back to those moments in the mine—the odd chill, the unearthly shadows, the ghostly miner with a history of tragedy. They had found the pendant and were promised luck, but Greg couldn't escape the feeling that what if their time in the mine was also a kind of warning? What if he was wrong about the ghostly miner's intentions, and instead, the jewelry carried a piece of that haunted past into their future together?

As much as he wanted this ring to represent his love and commitment to Libby, he couldn't help but wonder if the amethyst—bearing a spirit's blessing—might bring more than good fortune. Was it connected to the mine's dark past? Would that same mystery shadow their future?

He tried to shake it off, reminding himself of the joy they'd shared on their adventures. But that faint, lingering worry settled in the back of his consciousness, hinting that their story with the mine might not be over.

CHAPTER TWENTY-SEVEN

As I walked away from Alvarez's office, a strange feeling settled over me. I recognized that twinge from deep within. The one I sense when my trust had been broken. Trying to ignore it, I walked purposefully to my 4Runner, got in, and started it up. My eyes scanned the parking lot, although I couldn't quite place what I was looking for. I moved the gear into reverse, watching my backup camera as I carefully pulled out of the space.

I decided I'd pay my mom a visit this afternoon. She and Margie had been doing some church fundraiser activities lately, so I wasn't sure I'd find her at home, but thought I'd try, anyway. The day was cool with loads of sunshine. I picked up Shadow from home and then drove to my mother's neighborhood nearby, finding her outside on the front porch enjoying the sunshine with a mug of hot tea.

As soon as I opened the back door, Shadow bounded out and up to her grandmother. I grabbed my purse from the passenger seat and followed her.

"Hey, I wasn't expecting you today," she said pleasantly.

"Yeah, me either. But I was close by and thought I should check in."

"Well, now with those bad guys caught, you've dropped all that, right?"

I wasn't sure how much more I wanted to involve her. The warning was clear from Renee Alvarez … the danger still lurks and we had to keep a low profile.

"Well, it should be completed real soon."

She shook her head in disgust. "I still can't get over your father trying to bring them down … what was he thinking?"

"Probably that he was obeying the law and so should they."

"Want a cup of tea?" she asked.

"Sure, but don't get up. I'll go get it." Shadow followed me inside, beelined it straight for grandma's cookie jar and sat, staring up at me.

"Every time," I whispered, opening up the jar and pulled out a dog biscuit. "Good girl," I praised, throwing her a cookie.

I took a mug from the cabinet and found her selection of teas. The kettle on the stovetop had cooled, so I turned the dial to HI and waited for it to whistle. Shadow let out of low woof, standing up to the table, scratching one paw against the top.

"No, Shadow…down." She did as instructed, but her

nose pointed directly where her paw had been.

"What's this about?" I scratched the back of her head and she knocked my hand away, letting out another loud bark.

From a pile of mail that sat on her kitchen tabletop, I moved some papers around. My pup let out another bark and something caught my eye. It was the logo that stood out. I scooted aside another envelope and picked up the one with the swirls. H-W Amethyst. Why was my mother getting mail from this company? I peeked around the corner into her living room, where I could see through the screen door that she was still sipping on her mug on the front patio.

Taking some liberties, I slid my finger under the envelope's edge and quietly opened it. Unfolding the trifold insert, I pulled out what appeared to be an account summary. When I scanned down to the 'ending value', I nearly choked on my own saliva. There was over *three million dollars* in this investment account.

The tea kettle whistle caused me to jump. I quickly shut the stove off, poured my cup, and then hustled outside.

"Mom, how long have you been getting these?" I showed her the statement I was referring to.

Shaking her head, her eyes squinted as she looked at the paper. "I've never seen this before."

"Mom, it has your name on it and was sitting on your kitchen table. Three *million* dollars?" I whispered the last part, not wanting nosey neighbors overhearing.

"I suppose I thought it was junk mail—I sure get a lot of that. Certainly, there's some mistake. You know I don't have that kind of money." She turned the paper over, scrutinizing the company information. "And I've never heard of this company before in my life!"

"Not even from Dad when he worked at the insurance company?"

"No."

"I found this company mentioned in the paperwork from his files. From our investigative work, it seems to be a mining holding company."

"Well, I never…"

"May I?" I held my hand out, wanting to see the statement again.

After reading again through what appeared to be a legitimate document, I asked her one more time. "You've *never* seen anything from this company before today? Not even thinking it was junk mail and maybe throwing it away?"

"No, I don't think so." She shook her head adamantly.

"Okay, may I take this with me? I need to show it to the private investigators I'm working with."

She nodded and muttered, "Oh, I thought you were done with all that."

"Yeah, not completely. And I certainly don't want *this* dragging us back into it—we've got to be careful," I said. My hands shook as I tucked it into my purse.

We visited for another hour or more, but distractedly, I kept wondering where the statement came from out of the blue. Who sent it? Was it even legit? What if it was a ploy, somehow, to involve my mother in those thugs' illicit schemes? Somehow framing her, implicating her in their crimes? I couldn't imagine how, or why, but right now, I was skeptical and trusted no one.

CHAPTER TWENTY-EIGHT

On my way home, I called JJ and told him about what I'd found at my mother's. He was as perplexed as I was.

"Can you stop by on your way home?"

The moment Shadow and I entered the Johnson's house, she and Joshua ran off to their backyard and I only saw flashes of the kid's yellow jacket as they sped by the door, running around wildly.

Lexi offered me a glass of wine, which I gladly accepted.

JJ asked about Nathan's progress on getting enough evidence organized to get those hoodlums behind bars, once and for all. I filled him in on everything I knew so far and then pulled out the statement I found at my mother's home.

"I'm almost afraid of divulging this bit to the authorities," I said, taking another sip from my glass.

He looked it over and gave a long whistle as he pointed out the bottom line to Lexi. Their eyes were the size of saucers when they met mine again.

"I don't think you have to. And you say this is from the mining holding company?" he asked. "The same mine we visited?"

I nodded.

"Your mom had to have known about this account," Lexi added.

I shrugged. "Well, I believed her when she said she didn't. I mean, I think I'd know if my mom lied to my face."

JJ mumbled, "She's being set up."

My eyes flew open wide. "Yes! That's what I'm afraid of!"

"If it's legit, the police would have discovered this years back—at the time of his death."

"What if someone is trying to lure her into this mess? Muddy the waters…" Lexi started.

"Where there's no other record that the authorities would find," I finished.

Lexi nodded, looking at JJ for confirmation. He only shrugged.

I held up a finger, still shaking my head. "I don't understand the catch, though. Let's say they are trying to pin something on my mom. The account and money in it are legit and she tried to cash it out. Ultimately, a bank would have to fund it. Therefore, the feds would know. So, why expose themselves that way and end up giving Julia Madsen that much money?"

"Or if it's a scam, trying to lure her to them, then what?" Lexi asked.

"Yeah, exactly, that's what I don't understand, either. Something stinks. I suppose the only thing that makes sense is that they're funneling money around and are trying to implicate her somehow because of the mess her husband stirred up. But, why now?"

JJ nodded. "Maybe because you've stirred things up? I do think you're on to something; I'm just not sure what their game is. So, what do you want to do next?"

"Keep this between us for now. I'll tell Mom it's a scam; to forget about it and not to talk to anyone about what we've found."

"And then what?" Lexi asked, as she poured us more wine.

"Then we wait. Let's see if she receives more communications from H-W Amethyst. Maybe there's a way to track it? I can discuss it with Nathan and Renee."

My phone rang—it was Greg. We asked him to join us, and Lexi whipped up some dinner while we filled him in on all our findings.

By the time we got home that evening, Shadow had exhausted herself from all the activity with her five-year-old friend.

I wished I hadn't handed the files over to Alvarez—my mind was buzzing with questions and I wanted to rummage through folders looking for any evidence about this investment account.

Before joining Greg on the sofa for late night television, I checked my phone for messages. No texts and no missed calls. I found it strange that I hadn't heard from Nathan since he'd picked up the files several days ago. Fortunately,

Alvarez was keeping me apprised, but I felt unsettled at how silent Nathan had gone.

There was nothing I could do about it tonight, so I settled on the sofa next to Greg, reaching over and grabbing some popcorn from the bowl he held.

Sometime around midnight, we finally called it a night.

* * *

Several days passed before I heard anything further about the investigation. Still no word from Nathan and only a text message from Renee Alvarez basically telling me to settle down and they're handling things.

Greg saw my distress when he ventured into the kitchen for his coffee. He came over to the table where I sat and leaned over to kiss the top of my head. "You're stressing over something—out with it."

I turned around, looking up at him. "Oh, my private investigator has gone AWOL. Our newest ally is pushing me aside. Pretty sure they're both pushing me out."

"Well, maybe that's not all bad? They'll figure it all out and see that Peter Daniels and Detective Ross pay for their crimes. And maybe you and I can get back to finding fun excursions to go on when we're not working."

"Will they though?" I questioned. I stood up, pushing by Greg to pour myself another cup of coffee. "And what about that investment account my mom says she never set up?"

"Maybe you should call the number for the holding company and see what you can learn about it?"

I hadn't thought about that. "You know, that's a great idea. I'll get with Mom today." I checked my watch and realized I was running late to work.

"Sometimes I surprise even myself…" I heard him mutter as I darted out of the room.

* * *

Tony was waiting for me in the lobby when I stepped through the doors at Dharma Inspired Spa. Our receptionist, Cody, shot me an apologetic expression. Shadow barked and immediately gave Tony a thorough sniffing.

"Tony, I wasn't expecting you," I said pleasantly. "Did we have an appointment?"

"Libby, we need to talk. In private."

I glanced over to Cody and asked him if the office was free, which was really me asking whether Lexi had arrived to work yet. She hadn't, so I took Tony into our office.

"Please sit," I motioned toward the empty chair.

"Libby—I don't have a good feeling about all this."

"What exactly…"

"Listen, I gave my statement to Detective Alvarez. I don't think this is going the way you thought it would."

"What do you mean? What's the concern?"

"I just feel like I'm going straight to prison—with the rest of them."

"Did she say that?"

"No."

"Then … *what?* What did she say?"

He leaned in and whispered, "Libby, how well do you know her?"

"Alvarez? Well, I only recently met her, but she comes highly recommended from my private investigator. And he was working with my dad—I trust him." I left out the part where I felt he'd deserted me this week.

"Hmm. I have a strange feeling. It's bad enough that Rob isn't the friend I thought he was—man, I fell for his shenanigans, going along with research on the historical status of that mine site." He wrung his hands together, clearly stressed about something more than what he was saying. "Okay, so I talked to Rob again. I wasn't going to—because honestly, I'm terrified of the people he's involved with. I thought he'd listen."

"And did he?"

He shrugged noncommittally.

"Had you told him I'd come to you also asking about the historical status of the mine?"

He nodded.

"Okay, so he knows we're working together."

"Honestly, he warned me to watch my back and said something like 'not everyone is who you think they are'. And he followed it up with another ominous caution—something like, 'we're in over our heads'. Not those exact words, but that's what he meant."

"Uh, 'we' as in you and me? Or you and him?"

He shrugged. "Could be both, couldn't it?"

"And that's why you're asking me how well I know Nathan Pierce and Renee Alvarez?"

He nodded, casting his eyes downward.

"Remind me, how did you become involved with Rob again?"

"Old college buddy—but, Libby, honestly, I had no idea what he was involved with when he asked me to do the research work. And to tell you the truth, I think Rob was only trying to drum up investment business. At least at first; but clearly since then, he's caught up with the wrong crowd. I don't even recognize the person he's become."

As Tony talked, I remembered about Rob's investment banking background, but stayed quiet about that statement my mom received. One thing that was clear from this conversation—I needed to be careful with whom I trusted. It certainly wasn't Rob or Tony, whom I'd only casually known for a couple of weeks.

Once Tony had everything off his chest, his face relaxed a little more. He stood to leave right as Lexi tapped on the door.

"Libby, are you in?" she called out.

I got up to open the door, letting my guest out and my business partner in. They greeted one another, but Tony quickly made his way through the building and out the front door.

She turned to me. "What was that about?"

"Just when I thought everything would settle out—it only became more complicated."

CHAPTER TWENTY-NINE

Greg pulled up at Julia's house shortly after nine that morning. She was outside pruning her rose bush when her face broke out into a huge smile. She set down her pruning sheers and walked toward Greg as he approached on the walkway.

"Well, this is a surprise!" she exclaimed. "I'm so happy to see you, Greg. Come in, come in." She held open the front door and Greg walked through. "Can I get you some coffee or tea?"

"A cup of coffee, if you have a pot brewed already. Otherwise, water is fine." He took a seat at the kitchen table.

"Oh, I always have a pot on," she scoffed. She opened the cabinet and pulled out a mug, then poured from the decanter on her countertop. "What brings you by?"

"Well, I think tonight's the night, and I'm nervous. I guess since you're the only one who knows, I came by for some reassurance."

Julia set the mug down on the table in front of Greg. Quickly, she pulled out the chair next to his, sat down and touched his arm. "Tonight? You'll propose tonight?"

"You think that's a bad idea?"

"No!"

His eyes questioned hers.

Her hand flew up in front of her open mouth. "Oh! It's all coming together, *finally*." Tears welled up and she reached out again to squeeze his hand. "How are you going to do it? Are you taking her somewhere swanky? Or maybe you'll stay home for a nice, quiet evening? Or will the friends be around for it?" Her questions continued in rapid fire.

He held up a hand. "Whoa! Julia … easy." He chuckled, then took a sip of coffee. Then he reached into his jacket pocket and pulled out the little black box. "You know, I've carried this around with me more in the past several months … ever since Alaska, actually. I've been waiting for the exact right timing, and things keep happening. Now, I feel there will never be an optimal time, so I just need to do it."

He carefully opened the box, and Julia's eyes sparkled as bright as the diamond and amethysts. "Ohhh, she is going to *love* this. Are those…?"

His head was already nodding in answer to her noticing the addition of the amethysts. "I know she has a lot on her plate right now, with her father's death investigation and all."

"Oh, but I think the PI has taken over most of it. Don't

worry about that—just do it!" Her fingers reached out for the black box and he handed it over. She turned the box, admiring the ring from different angles, and becoming giddy with delight over the sparkling effects made by the overhead lights catching the gems just so.

"That's what I was hoping you'd say. I don't want to be disrespectful to her, or to you, by distracting with a proposal when there's more important business. But I sensed it was wrapping up as well."

"I can't imagine there's much more she'll be involved with—I think it's all with the legal system now."

He smiled, hearing everything he wanted. They shared more conversation over coffee before he had to leave for work.

* * *

I walked out of the massage room and immediately checked my phone for missed calls. I had several messages in to Nathan by now and really wanted to talk to him about my earlier conversation with Tony. The only missed call was from Greg—he had left a message saying he'd bought some steaks and had a nice dinner planned for us at home. My heart swelled.

Lexi walked into the office and smiled. "If only I could capture that exact expression on you more often. What were you just thinking, my friend?" she asked.

I waggled my phone. "Oh, Greg's fixing dinner. I really love getting messages like that."

"Yes! JJ surprises me every now and then, too." She pulled out her keyboard tray and typed in her password. Her eyes found mine again. "You never said why Tony was here earlier."

I sighed. "I'm still trying to figure it all out. And I'm not so sure I can completely trust him."

"Well, we know for sure we can't trust Rob—so I imagine you're correct."

"And I can't get hold of Nathan. That has me worried, since he's really the only one I know is on my dad's side."

Her face said it all. "Oh…"

"Yeah. Let's just say that I'm sufficiently worried."

"I'm sure he'll surface again soon. He's busy."

"Now Tony has me worried—saying I can't trust anyone. Including Nathan and Renee. I can't imagine why since they helped my father years back. Well, Nathan did anyway. I trust him."

"Jesus, Libby. It has gotten complicated, hasn't it?"

I nodded. My phone chirped, and Nathan's name on the display caught my attention. I punched the icon for my text messages and read:

Sorry Libby. Crazy busy. We'll talk soon.

"That's it?" I muttered.

Lexi looked concerned. "Maybe Renee has been in touch? Or could help you—?"

I silently nodded as I typed a message back to Nathan, asking him to look into Tony's background more. I also shot off a message about the investment fund information found at my mom's house. Although I hadn't wanted to have that conversation via text messaging, I also thought it would be helpful if my private investigator could work on researching those two pieces before we talked.

I looked back up at Lexi. "Hey, I've got to run a few errands before my next appointment. I'll let you know what I find out when Nathan responds." I grabbed my purse and headed out to my car.

The rest of the afternoon flew by and before I knew it, I was scrambling to get home after a couple of text messages from Greg asking whether he should put the steaks on yet.

CHAPTER THIRTY

The warm glow of candles flickered across the room as Greg set the table with precision. A small bouquet of wildflowers sat in the center, next to a bottle of wine he'd been saving for the special occasion. He wiped his hands on a towel, checking the steaks searing in the cast-iron skillet. The scent of garlic and rosemary filled the air, mingling with the soft strains of jazz playing from a speaker in the corner.

Libby walked into the kitchen, Shadow padding at her heels. She was in a cozy sweater and leggings, her hair loose around her shoulders. "Wow," she said, taking in the scene. "This looks *incredible*."

Greg smiled, his hands slightly shaky as he plated the steaks alongside roasted vegetables and a side of mashed potatoes. "I thought we deserved a pleasant night in."

Libby leaned over and kissed his cheek. "You're spoiling me."

As they sat down, Greg filled their glasses and raised his. "To us. For surviving mines, tough hikes, and a very turbulent helicopter ride."

Libby laughed, clinking her glass to his. "I'll drink to that."

They talked and giggled over dinner; the conversation flowed effortlessly, but Greg's nerves buzzed. Was it the right time? Was she ready? What if the ring's history made this all wrong?

After they finished, Libby leaned back with a satisfied sigh. "Okay, that might be the best steak I've ever had. What's the occasion?"

Greg nervously cleared his throat while standing and moving toward the sideboard. "You could say it's … uh, a culmination of a lot of things."

She tilted her head curiously as he returned to her side, holding a small box in his hand.

"Libby," he began, his voice shaken. "I had this whole elaborate plan during our trip to Four Peaks. Then again, at Canyon Lake. But every time, something else got in the way. And maybe that was for the best, because tonight feels like the perfect moment."

Her eyes widened as he knelt before her, opening the box to reveal the stunning ring—a delicate band set with a sparkling diamond and the amethysts they'd retrieved from the mine.

"Oh my God," she whispered, her hand covering her mouth.

"Libby, you make me feel like the luckiest man in the

world. Every adventure, every challenge—it all feels worth it because you're by my side. Will you marry me?"

Tears streamed down her face as she nodded, unable to find the words at first. Finally, she managed, "Yes! Yes, of course!"

He slipped the ring onto her finger, and she threw her arms around him, laughing through her tears. Shadow barked excitedly, circling around them in delight.

As they pulled apart, Libby looked down at the ring, her gaze fixating on the amethysts. "It's beautiful. But Greg, do you think this will raise questions?"

Greg's shoulders stiffened slightly. "I've been thinking about that too," he admitted, kicking himself for rushing to the jeweler without question. "We know it was given to us when we helped release the trapped souls, but proving that is something entirely different. The last thing I want is for someone to think we took it from the mine without permission."

Libby frowned, delicately touching the stone with her thumb. "I hadn't thought about that. Do you think there's a way to prove it?"

"It's possible," Greg said, his brows furrowed. "I promise you; we'll do the right thing. But honestly, I'd rather deal with all of that than not have this moment with you now."

Libby smiled softly, her fingers curling around his. "We'll figure it out. For now, I just want to enjoy this. Did you design this?"

"Well, I had a concept ... but no, I had help. And we'll work with him if we need to make adjustments, depending on how everything settles out."

"I trust you. This is one of the sweetest things anyone

has ever done for me." Libby tiptoed to reach his lips; her arms lovingly snaked around his neck.

Greg's shoulders eased as he leaned in, kissing her, the enormity of their concerns momentarily lifting.

As they sat on the couch, wine glasses in hand, Libby's expression changed. "Do you think there's a chance these stones connect to the case?"

Greg's jaw tightened. "Maybe. If they do, it could either help us prove your dad's connection or it might complicate things even more."

Libby sighed, her tenacity wavering. "Looks like we've got more digging to do. But not tonight. Tonight, we celebrate." Her eyes lifted to meet his. Smiling, she leaned over and kissed him.

Greg grinned, relieved. He lifted his glass. "To us. And to mysteries we can tackle *after* the wedding."

Libby laughed, clinking her glass to his. "Deal."

Shadow settled on her bed in the corner of the living room, and for the moment, all other problems stayed in the background. They both looked forward to their future together, excitedly planning the beginning of another chapter.

* * *

The next morning, I couldn't stop admiring the gems resting on my ring finger. We sat on the sofa on our back porch, Shadow busily wandering around the yard. The early rising sun painted the Arizona sky in streaks of yellow and pink, and a light breeze rustled through the desert plants. I leaned back against Greg, nestled between his legs, my hand absently tracing the outline of the princess-cut diamond and amethyst engagement ring.

"So," I began with a dreamy smile, "have you ever thought about what your dream wedding would look like?"

Greg chuckled, resting his chin on my shoulder. "Honestly? I didn't think I'd ever get married, so I haven't spent much time picturing it. But now … yeah, I have some ideas."

I tilted my head to look up at him. "Oh? Do tell."

"Well," he said, his voice thoughtful, "I'd love to have it somewhere outdoors, with lots of open space. Maybe a forest clearing or a field with a view of the mountains. Something simple and natural."

I smiled, turning my attention back to the horizon. "I like that. No fancy banquet halls or stuffy ballrooms. Just fresh air and a view that makes everyone feel like they're part of something magical."

Greg nodded. "Exactly. And maybe we could time it so the ceremony happens just before sunset, with all those colors in the sky. Imagine saying our vows with the sun dipping behind the mountains."

"That sounds perfect," I softly said. "What about decorations? You know, the stuff people usually obsess over."

Greg laughed. "I'm not exactly an expert on decorations, but I figure we'd keep it simple. Some wildflowers, maybe string lights or lanterns for when it gets dark. Enough to enhance the setting without taking away from it."

I sighed happily. "You're so much better at this than I thought you'd be."

"Hey, I've had a lot of practice thinking about the perfect moment for the engagement," he teased. "Proposals and weddings go hand in hand, right?"

I laughed, nudging him playfully. "What about the food? You know our families will expect a feast."

"Oh, definitely," Greg agreed. "We could do something casual but amazing—like a big outdoor barbecue or a catered spread of local favorites. Maybe even a combination of your family's traditions and mine."

"That's a good idea," I said, feeling that swell of excitement. "And for dessert? Not just a wedding cake. We could have a dessert table with all kinds of treats—pies, cookies, maybe s'mores if there's a fire pit."

Greg grinned. "I like the way you think, Mrs. Lawson."

Looking up at him again, I smiled upon hearing my soon-to-be new name spoken aloud.

"And speaking of fire pits, what if we ended the night with everyone gathered around, sharing stories and toasting marshmallows under the stars?"

My eyes lit up. "Yes! That's perfect. It's like a celebration of us but also of everything we love—family, nature, adventure."

We sat in comfortable silence for a moment, the vision of the wedding coming to life in our minds. Shadow stirred, stretching before resting her head on Greg's foot.

"You know," I added, "wherever we have it, as long as we're together, it'll be perfect."

Greg kissed the top of my head. "You took the words right out of my mouth."

My phone rang and I groaned. I wasn't in the mood to go back into real life yet. I loved our dream state, but I begrudgingly sat up and grabbed the phone from the nearby coffee table. Looking at the display, I saw it was my mom. Greg's smile caught my attention.

"What?" I teased.

"She's probably expecting a call from you."

"She knows?"

He motioned his hand for me to hurry and pick up the call. I punched the button.

Mom sounded chipper. "Good morning!"

"Hi Mom." I smiled at Greg, deciding I'd drag this out.

"How was your evening?" she asked surreptitiously.

"Fine. How was yours?"

She gave a harrumph. "Good, but how was your *nice steak dinner*, honey? Anything to report?"

"It was great—Greg is so good with steaks, isn't he? I'd say it was medium…"

"Libby!"

I laughed and Greg hollered out, "She said yes!"

"Oh! I'm so happy," my mom squealed and I could picture her eyes were probably filling with tears. "It's about time!"

Between the two of them, they started telling me more missed opportunity proposal tales. I sat there with my mouth gaping open, clueless about *how long* this had gone on.

"In Alaska you were going to propose?" I asked him, looking down at the ring. "But…"

He filled my mom and me in on the entire story about the jeweler and taking the already-purchased diamond ring to have a jeweler design in the special amethysts. I was stunned at how much he'd done behind the scenes that I was completely unaware of, and prayed we wouldn't have to deconstruct the amethyst gems from the beautiful setting.

I noticed on the screen that Nathan's name popped up. "Oh no, Mom … I need to call you back. I've got to take this call."

I stood up, frantically trying to retrieve Nathan's

call before he hung up. Walking back inside the house, I answered, "Nathan, I'm so glad you called."

"Libby. Listen to me. We need to get your mother to a safe place quickly. She's in danger."

In a few broad strokes, he began to outline a plan.

CHAPTER THIRTY-ONE

Stepping up onto the walkway in front of the decades old shopping center, I turned my head back to the parking lot, making sure I wasn't being followed. I glanced around, looking for Nathan's vehicle, but couldn't spot it.

Impatience was brewing inside me. Why had he moved? None of this made sense. I continued down the sidewalk, trying to find unit number 210, and realized I'd parked at the wrong end of the expansive property. Thirty-eight, Forty-two … I sped up, now speed-walking toward the other end where I hoped I'd find the two-hundreds.

The parking lot wasn't full. In fact, I wondered how many of the businesses were still operational. Many were vacant, but I saw several: a tattoo parlor, a hair salon, a water and ice storefront, as well as a tax preparation center, that would probably open up later in the morning. What a strange location for a private investigator to set up shop. Of course, maybe that was the purpose: to *not* bring attention. And it explained why I hadn't heard from him for days—he was in the process of moving, apparently.

Rounding a corner, I finally found the suite number I was looking for. There was no business name on the door; I used my hands to shield my eyes, trying to peer inside the dark tinted glass. It was empty. *What kind of wild-goose chase was this?*

Just then, I heard a click in the door lock and jumped back. The door opened, and I saw Renee smiling. "You found me," she said.

Confused, I looked behind me one more time before stepping over the threshold. "Is Nathan here yet?"

"He'll be along shortly." She quickly prompted me inside.

I saw her eyes scan the corridor outside the office too, before quickly closing the door behind her and clicking the lock into place.

Something was off, but I couldn't precisely place it. Perhaps it was simply the fact that we were going to move my mother. I couldn't imagine why anyone would go after her.

Renee walked me through the empty storefront and into a small office near the rear of the building. She pulled out a chair, indicating I should sit, before she rounded the desk and took her seat in Nathan's black leather executive's chair.

"We have the credentials ready…" She handed me an identification card with my mother's picture on it.

"Is all this really necessary?" I asked, reading the card

which read: Sally Fromen.

"We can never be too careful." Renee cleared her throat before opening the desk drawer and pulling out another piece of paper. "Here are her boarding passes. You're sure this is the safest place we could stash her?"

I winced, hearing her refer to my mother as some random disposable object, but I nodded. "No one should connect her with Greg's family, since they've only recently come into our lives."

I'm not sure Renee was convinced, but we really had no other choice at the moment. Anne and Bill Lawson lived in rural Colorado—she should be safer there until this was over.

I checked my watch; we were running out of time. I needed to get my mom on that plane. "Listen, I expected to meet with Nathan and I really need to talk to him. Shouldn't he be here by now?"

Her eyes met mine. For a second, there was that indiscernible glint I'd seen from her before. Then she smiled widely. "I'm sure he overslept—it wouldn't be the first time." She stood, brushing by me and opening the office door. "You best be off now."

* * *

Julia Madsen hurriedly packed her carry-on bag. From the closet, she pulled out an oversized down jacket—the same one she'd taken on their Alaska cruise months earlier.

When I walked into her room, she looked frazzled. "I just don't understand why they need me there now. I can't believe we're not throwing you an engagement party. Everyone needs to know!"

"I know. It feels rushed, but really, you're helping us all out. And, don't worry, soon enough, we'll gather all the friends and announce our engagement."

She did not look pacified. "And why the fake name?"

"Mom, you need to stop calling it that." I took her gently by the shoulders and stared directly into her eyes. "Please. I can't tell you everything—for your own safety. Trust me and everything will be fine. You *have* to be Sally while you're traveling." I pulled a phone from my pocket. "Here's a new phone, with numbers already programmed in. They are the only ones you can use—mine, Greg's, and his parents."

Her forehead wrinkled. "I can't call Jordan and check in on the kids?"

"No. But honestly, this won't be long at all. Promise. And besides, Greg's parents are eager to see you."

"I just don't understand anything that's going on here..." she repeated.

"And let's keep it that way, okay?"

"Is it about that money we found?"

"Don't speak of that to *anyone*. Forget we ever found that investment paperwork—it's probably fake anyhow."

Her eyes squinted, giving me her classic skeptical look. Finally, she reached out and hugged me. "I'm not sure what you've gotten yourself involved in this time, but you better resolve it quickly. It's cold in Colorado this time of year."

I grabbed her thermal jacket and picked up the suitcase. "Look around and see if there's anything else." I stopped her when she reached for the phone sitting on her dresser. "Do not take that—leave it here. You have all your medications?"

She nodded and followed me to the front of the house.

As I loaded up the car, she went around securing all doors and windows, making sure her home was safe.

Questions filled our drive to the airport, and I couldn't answer most of them. I felt horrible for this turmoil in her life right now, but above all else, I'd do anything to keep her safe.

"Anne and Bill will be at the Denver airport waiting for you just outside the security area."

"But I thought Anne needed help to get around after her fall."

Oops. "Well, maybe it'll be Bill and Dana then. I'm not sure. But you know Greg's family—only go with them. No one else."

A wave of apprehension washed over me, wondering if my mother would follow all the instructions. And there was the whole other part of me that questioned whether it was even necessary. It felt as though I didn't have a choice though—I was following Nathan and Renee's instructions. Anything to keep my family safe. And what had she kept telling me—*keep a low-profile, Libby.* Along with that ominous warning of retaliation.

CHAPTER THIRTY-TWO

From the airport, I drove directly to the spa. I had a difficult time getting the image of my mother's final expression out of my thoughts. I'd walked her to the security line and waved as she joined the throngs of people. Hesitating while I watched her make her way to the front of the line, I saw her hand over her identification, smile when the TSA agent handed it back to her, and she lugged her suitcase to the security conveyor for scanning. That's when she turned and faced my direction. The worry etched across her face made tears form in my eyes. She didn't see me, but I watched her go through the scanning device and that's when I lost sight of her.

Now, pulling up in front of my business, I wiped away the tears and geared myself up for a full day's work and the announcement. I'd called ahead to find out which of my colleagues were there today. The entire crew was there, and Cody said if I hurried, I'd catch Bella there too since she drove him today.

As I walked through the front door, the soft hum of instrumental music and the soothing scent of lavender heightened the spa's serene ambiance. No one was in the front lobby yet; it was early, about an hour before opening.

I called out and asked the employees—all dear friends—to join me in the Serenity Room. Lexi, Bella, Cody, Diane, and Kathleen strolled in one by one, chatting and carrying their usual warm energy into the room.

Shadow came running out of our office when she heard my voice. I thanked Lexi for picking her up on her way in.

"This place always feels like a sanctuary," Diane said, inhaling deeply. "I feel calmer just walking through the door, and how long have I worked here now? Well over a year, for sure."

"Hey, Libby!" Bella exclaimed. "It's been a while. There's so much to catch up on."

I smiled, barely able to contain my excitement. "Yes, there certainly is."

Lexi tilted her head, intrigued. "Oh? What's going on?"

Cody plopped down on the comfortable sofa, grinning. "You're practically glowing, Lib. Spill it!"

I couldn't hold back any longer. I held up my left hand, my face breaking into a radiant smile. The group collectively gasped as the light caught the dazzling diamond and amethyst ring.

"I'm engaged!" I announced.

The spa erupted into a chorus of cheers and excited chatter from my colleagues. Shadow let out a cheerful bark, bouncing up and hitting me with her front paws enthusiastically.

"Oh my gosh, it's gorgeous!" Bella exclaimed, rushing over to get a closer look. "Those amethysts—so unique!"

Lexi grabbed my hand, studying the ring with wide eyes. "Wait. Is this …?"

I nodded, grinning. "Yes! Greg had it custom-made. He said he wanted something special, something that would always remind me of that adventure."

They laughed heartily as I told them the stories, dating back months, and all the times he attempted to propose. Even though it hadn't happened on some grand adventure, my heart warmed thinking about all he'd gone through to carry out his plans.

"Leave it to Greg to think of something so thoughtful," Kathleen said warmly.

"Okay, this is officially the most romantic engagement ever," Diane declared. "And this ring? It's a showstopper."

Cody laughed. "Oh dear, Greg set a high standard for all of us, hasn't he?"

I playfully hit his arm. "You're already married. And talk about romantics—you and Brad!"

"Well," Bella interjected, "this calls for a toast, even if it's herbal tea!"

I giggled and darted into the nearby kitchen. I opened the cupboard and pulled out glasses, shouting back to the group, "Actually, I made a lavender and honey mocktail. Figured it would fit the vibe." Thankfully, it was a concoction I'd made a batch of the day before. Unfortunately, or fortunately, I completely forgot about it when Greg served wine and champagne at my surprise steak dinner last night. As I poured the cups, I smiled thinking it was much better suited for this moment, anyway.

The group gathered in the spa's lounge, clinking glasses as Diane raised hers. "To Libby and Greg! May your marriage be as beautiful and unique as this ring."

"To Libby and Greg!" the others echoed.

I felt my cheeks flush as they all smiled at me, their love and support filling the room.

As the chatter continued, Lexi leaned closer. "So, when's the big day? Are we thinking small, like the spa, or something more extravagant?"

"We have some ideas for an outdoor wedding, but I have no idea *when*," I admitted, laughing. "I'm still just wrapping my head around being engaged!"

"Well, you've got us to help when the time comes," Cody said, smiling.

I nodded, taking it all in. My friends, the spa, and this new chapter in my life—it all felt surreal. Shadow, lounging in her bed off to the side of us, let out a soft woof, as if reminding everyone she was part of the moment, too.

"Don't worry, sweet girl," I said, looking over at her. "You'll be every bit a part of it, too."

Everyone laughed; the joy in the room was unmistakable.

CHAPTER THIRTY-THREE

Several days went by. I hadn't heard a word from either Nathan or Renee. I had checked in with Mom at the Lawson's a few times each day and she was having a great time with Anne, although she questioned me often on exactly why she was there. After a couple of days, it didn't matter. She had enjoyed baking several yummy things with my future mother-in-law, and she spoke of a new stew recipe she'd have to make for the family when she returned home.

This particular morning, I sat at the kitchen table scrolling through the day's news headlines on my phone when I heard Greg beginning to stir in the other room. The sun cast a golden glow through the kitchen window as I got up to refresh my coffee and pour him a mug. Shadow lay sprawled on the floor, tail thumping lazily. Greg walked in, still groggy, rubbing his neck.

"Morning," he mumbled, leaning over to kiss my cheek.

"Morning," I replied, handing him a mug. "I made the good stuff today."

He smiled, taking a sip. "Bless you."

Before we could settle into our usual morning banter, Greg's phone buzzed on the counter. He glanced at the screen, his brows furrowing. "It's my supervisor."

"Everything okay?" I asked, concerned.

Greg shrugged, picking up the call. "Hey, Dave. What's up?"

I watched as Greg's relaxed posture stiffened. He turned toward the window, his voice dropping to a serious tone.

"Silver City? Yeah, I've been there before. What's going on?" He listened intently, nodding occasionally. "A big storm? Trees down? Okay, when do you need me?"

Disappointment set in as I listened to his side of the conversation.

"Got it. I'll head out this afternoon. Thanks for letting me know." Greg hung up and turned back to me, an apologetic look spread across his face.

"I have to go," he said.

"Let me guess—storm damage in Silver City?"

"Yeah, you caught all that. A storm tore through the area last night and the NM forestry crews are short-handed right now. Anyway, they need all hands on deck to clear the roads and assess the damage, and my division has been called in to assist."

"For how long?"

"Not really sure yet. Hopefully, only a night or two. They've got some remote homes that are cut off entirely, so we'll see how extensive it really is."

I nodded, trying to mask my disappointment. "That's important work. I get it."

Greg stepped closer, wrapping his arms around me. "I hate leaving you, especially with everything going on. Have you heard anything more from Nathan?"

I shook my head in answer to his question. "Hey, don't worry about all that. I'll be fine," I assured him. "This is your job, and it sounds like they really need you."

"I'll call every night," he promised.

"You better," I said with a small smile, trying to lighten the mood.

As Greg started gathering his gear, I watched, already missing him, but proud of the work he did. Shadow padded over to him, tail wagging, as if she understood that her favorite human was heading out. She probably also couldn't understand why her gear wasn't being gathered. Now, with her search and rescue certification, she understood the drill when Greg packed up his truck.

"Don't worry, girl," Greg said, giving Shadow a quick scratch behind the ears. "I'll be back before you know it. And next time; I'm sure there'll be a job for you."

And with that, Greg headed out, leaving me to sip my coffee and wonder what adventures—or challenges— might await him in the mountains of New Mexico.

* * *

After work, I stopped by to check on my mom's house. Everything looked normal and as we'd left it. Driving home, I picked up a pizza. Tonight, I wanted to dive in and learn more about that investment fund. Feeling left out of the investigation suddenly, I needed to keep myself busy, keep things moving along. There was something I was missing; I was sure of it. With the house quiet for a couple of days, I hoped reviewing my notes would bring a sudden brilliant epiphany.

Shadow had other ideas when I walked through the front door and set the pizza on the countertop. She'd been cooped up all day inside at the spa. We definitely needed a walk; the pizza could be reheated.

The evening breeze was chilly; I zipped up my insulated running jacket. Shadow was already pulling at me to get a move on. As we left the front entryway and made our way across the driveway and out onto the sidewalk, I saw Robin. I hadn't seen my neighbor in some time, and after some recent neighborhood events, which hadn't ended too well for her family, Greg and I figured they'd moved after her husband wound up in trouble with the law.

She waved, so I gave a wave back, and steered Shadow down the street the opposite way. Yes, maybe it was rude, and I have been curious about how Robin and the kids were doing, but that lady was a talker. I really wanted to avoid getting caught up in her chatter. Plus, there was a small part of me that wondered whether she blamed me for the mess they were in. I'd rather avoid that scrutiny.

We walked around a couple of blocks and snuck back home; thankfully, no one was outside at the neighbor's house when we returned.

After devouring several slices of pizza, I sat at the kitchen table with my laptop, scrolling through notes on my father's case while Shadow dozed in the corner.

Suddenly, my sleeping pup jolted awake, running for the front door, barking ferociously. Then came the knock at the door which startled me. I checked my watch—ten after six.

"Shadow, quiet." I walked to the door and squinted out the peephole. It was Nathan Pierce standing there, his usual confident demeanor wrapped in an unusual edge of tension.

"One moment!" I yelled, grabbing Shadow's collar and leading her to the kennel at the far end of the room. She resisted me and I struggled for several minutes to contain her before I walked back to the door.

"Nathan," I said, opening the door. "I wasn't expecting you." Shadow went ballistic in her crate.

"Shadow. Quiet!" I yelled. Then I turned back to Nathan. "I'm sorry about that. Come in."

"Thought I'd swing by," he said, stepping inside and closing the door behind him. His sharp eyes darted around the room, in search of the ferocious barker.

I gestured to a chair at the kitchen table, where I had my laptop set up. "Have a seat. I've been trying to reach you. I've been going through some leads we'd been working on, and there's—"

Nathan held up a hand. "Libby, listen. I need you to put a pin in reaching out to me directly for a while."

"What? Why?"

"I've had to move on to … other things," he said vaguely, avoiding my gaze. "For now, I need you to work with Renee. She'll pick up where I left off."

I blinked, my stomach tightening. "Renee? But I thought…"

"She knows everything," Nathan said, his tone clipped.

"That's not good enough, Nathan," I said, crossing my arms. "You've been the one guiding me through this. Why would you completely hand it off to someone else now, when we're so close to uncovering something big? Plus, she's gone absent nearly as much as you have lately. I need to know what the next steps are."

Nathan exhaled sharply, running a hand through his hair. "It's complicated, Libby. Let's just say I've got my own fires to put out, and I can't split my attention."

"Is that why you moved offices? Is someone pressuring you?" I asked, narrowing my eyes. "What kind of trouble are you in?"

Nathan chuckled, but it lacked humor. "You're asking the wrong questions."

"Am I?" I shot back, raising my voice. "Because from where I'm standing, you're being cryptic as hell, and it's making me wonder if I even know you at all. I thought you wanted to help *my father*?"

His jaw tightened, and for a moment, I thought he might actually answer. Instead, he stood and adjusted his coat. "Renee has my full confidence. She'll be in touch."

Shadow's barking pierced our ears. I shushed her again.

"That's it? You're just walking away?"

Nathan paused at the door, his hand on the knob. "Sometimes, stepping away is the best way to protect the people involved."

"Protect them from what? Nathan, if there's something you're not telling me—"

But he was already halfway out the door. "Take care, Libby."

As the front door clicked shut, Shadow kept pawing at her kennel door; I opened it for her and she ran, barking, toward the entryway.

I sank back into my chair, my mind racing once again.

After sniffing everywhere Nathan had been, Shadow sat on my feet, lifting her head to look at me as if sensing my unease.

"I don't like this, girl," I murmured, reaching down to scratch her ears. "I don't know what he's hiding, but something doesn't feel right."

Shadow wagged her tail, her dark eyes dutifully on mine, offering silent comfort.

I leaned back, staring at the closed door. I'd trusted Nathan. That is, up until now, anyway. His sudden departure left me with more questions than answers—and a sinking feeling that I had no idea who I could rely on.

CHAPTER THIRTY-FOUR

The next morning, I was halfway through folding a basket of laundry when my phone rang. Shadow, curled up nearby, lifted her head lazily but didn't budge.

I picked up the phone and saw Jordan's name on the screen.

"Hey, Jordan," I answered cheerfully, tucking the phone between my shoulder and ear.

"Libby, have you heard from Mom?" Jordan's voice was sharp, tinged with concern.

I froze for half a second before resuming the folding. "Why? Is something wrong?"

"I don't know! I've been calling her all day, and she's not answering. I even tried texting, but nothing. She always has her phone on her, Libby."

I couldn't tell Jordan the truth—that we'd sent our mom to stay with Greg's family in Colorado for a while. She couldn't know about the warnings that Mom's life was in danger. And I really didn't want to get into the subject of our concern over the investment account our mother knew nothing about. We'd tell Jordan what she needed to know when we learned the facts.

"I'm sure she's fine," I said, keeping my tone light. "She might just be busy. You know how she gets when she's running errands or cleaning the house. She probably didn't hear her phone."

"Libby," Jordan said, suspicious now. "She always calls me back. *Always.* And I can't even see her on Find My Friends. Did she say something to you about going somewhere?"

I hesitated, choosing my words carefully. "She might have mentioned wanting some quiet time."

"Quiet time? Where?"

"I ... don't know exactly," I lied smoothly. "Maybe she just needed to unplug for a bit. You know, step away from everything for a few days. She's been stressed lately."

Jordan was quiet for a moment. "You don't think she's avoiding me, do you? Because of that argument we had last week?"

I jumped on that opportunity. "That could be it," I said, my voice soothing. "She might just need some space. You know how she gets when things get tense. Give her a day or two, and I'm sure she'll reach out."

Jordan sighed; her frustration evident. "I guess. But if you hear from her before I do, let me know, okay?"

"Of course," I promised. "And don't worry. Mom's fine. She's just taking a little time for herself."

After Jordan hung up, I set the phone down with a sigh. I hated keeping secrets from Jordan, but I had no choice.

Shadow slunk over, leaning into my leg, and then she sat on my foot. I scratched her ears absentmindedly. "You're a good girl for not spilling secrets," I murmured. Shadow wagged her tail, her loyalty unwavering.

When my phone rang again, I groaned. *C'mon, Jordan.* I picked it up and saw it was JJ instead. Suddenly, my attention shifted. JJ rarely called unless it was important. I swiped to answer.

"JJ? What's up?"

"Libby," JJ's voice was low, cautious. "I need to talk to you about the investigation. Do you have a minute?"

"Of course. What's going on?" I muted the TV, then paced with anticipation.

JJ let out a shaky breath. "I think I've hit a wall at work. I've been digging into this and some leads we've talked about, but someone's caught on. Things are being ... um, how should I put it, *redirected.*"

"Redirected?" I repeated.

"Yeah. Someone has deleted the emails I sent to follow up on records. Also, someone flagged the requests I made through official channels. And just this afternoon, my supervisor pulled me aside for a *friendly chat* about staying focused on current cases."

"Oh no," I murmured. Shadow lifted her head, sensing my wariness. Her eyes followed me as I stood to pace around the room.

JJ hesitated before continuing. "As much as you've tried to protect me and keep Alvarez from knowing I'm assisting you, she must know. How else do you think my supervisor got involved? She *has* to be the one who contacted him."

"Do you think your job's at risk?"

JJ gave a bitter chuckle. "Not sure. I've worked hard to keep this under the radar, but if they've figured out that I'm nosing around, yeah, it could be. Worse, though, I might not be able to dig any deeper without risking further exposure."

I tightened my grip on the phone. "JJ, this is serious. Are you safe? Do you think they'd retaliate?"

"Who knows?" JJ admitted. "You know I've been careful. Anyway, I only wanted to give you a heads-up."

"Hey, do you want me to back off for now?" I asked.

"No," JJ said firmly. "We can't let this go. But I might call in a favor from Nathan—you know, since he's in the private sector."

"Uh, yeah. Just thinking that might be a problem."

"Why? What do you mean?"

"Nathan was here last night. He's bailed and left everything to Renee Alvarez."

"You're kidding me."

"Afraid not. And JJ, that's probably how Alvarez would know you're snooping around in the department. Nathan certainly could have mentioned your name along the way."

"Of course," he sighed. "We should have thought of that sooner, but we also don't know for sure she's the one causing trouble for me. Anyway, I'll keep you posted. For now, be prepared in case this gets … uh, any messier."

"Messier?"

JJ exhaled slowly. "Well, with the heat on Ross now, and whoever else is behind the cover-up, it wouldn't surprise me if it soon gets much more complicated. We've got to watch our backs."

The call ended, leaving me staring at my phone, my thoughts spinning. Shadow whined softly, nudging my hand.

I gave her a reassuring pat. "It's okay, sweetie. At least, I hope it is."

CHAPTER THIRTY-FIVE

By the next morning, I was losing my mind. No return calls from Alvarez. Nathan had indeed disappeared—I even drove by his office, trying to get him to reconsider. I'd been through all the notes that I'd kept, and seriously wished I hadn't given everything else to Renee.

Going through my daily chores, my therapy work at the spa, and taking Shadow out for runs wasn't cutting it anymore. I was a bundle of nerves, looking over my shoulders, and wanting the perpetrators back behind bars. I couldn't escape the feeling of impending doom.

When my phone rang and I saw it was Greg, my spirits lifted.

"Hey, honey! Everything going well in Silver City?"

Static sounds had me picturing him standing outdoors.

"Oh yeah, we made significant progress yesterday," he answered. "In fact, I don't want to get my hopes up too high, but I think we may return our unit to Arizona as early as tomorrow."

"Oh! That would be fantastic."

"Yeah, so what else is going on there? Everything good?"

I'd already explained that I announced our engagement to the spa employees, which of course included our friends, Lexi and JJ. We talked about having a dinner with the group of friends to celebrate when he returned.

"So, what news is there with the investigation?" he asked.

I updated him on my interaction with Nathan and then also JJ's concerns. We agreed about being worried about JJ's career—he should drop his involvement; it was simply not worth it. Greg was surprised about Nathan bailing on me.

"I don't know. The more I think about it—the police are working the angle with Ross and Daniels—maybe there isn't much more than that? Maybe it's okay that Nathan has other work to do and he's out? But there's something that still doesn't sit right with me. Like, the fact that I drove by his office yesterday and it's completely cleared out."

"Really?" The concern was rich in Greg's voice.

"I can understand him moving on to other investigations, but to move completely out of the office? Seemingly overnight? Twice, in short order!"

"Yeah, I agree with you. There's something going on there."

I heard several male voices shouting in the background. The sound of vehicles firing up was even louder.

"Listen, sweetie, I've gotta go. I'll call you tonight and

hopefully with good news that I'm headed home. I love you."

"Love you, too. Be safe!"

* * *

Later, when Renee *finally* returned my phone calls from days earlier, I couldn't hide my impatience. I demanded answers. What was she, or the police department, doing to protect those whom Ross and Daniels may try to pursue?

"I feel like we are sitting ducks!" I shouted. "Tell me, how much longer must my mother remain in Colorado?"

Renee shushed me, making me feel like a five-year-old child. Okay, maybe I was behaving like one, but I felt as though I had to get her attention.

"Libby, things like this take time. We're doing everything we can. I have a whole team on it."

I took a deep breath. Trying to manage my tone, I gritted my teeth and asked, "How sure are you that Daniels and Ross are going to be arrested? And where is Nathan?"

Renee's frustration was palpable. "Well, first we've got to locate them. And as for Nathan, he's working on another investigation now. You'll be working with me exclusively from now on. I thought he told you?"

I nodded compliantly. "Yes, I know. And I'm not thrilled about it, and hoped it wasn't true." I let out a pent-up breath. "Renee, it's just that Mom's already going stir-crazy in Colorado. Do you have any idea how much longer she'll have to be there?" I wanted to mention that my sister was asking questions, but didn't want to bring Jordan into her focus, either.

"Listen, I've already told you. Let me do my job—it

shouldn't be much longer."

My nerves buzzed and I quickly retorted, "I'd like my dad's files back."

Pure silence penetrated the air for an uncomfortable minute. "Libby…"

"I'm dead serious, Renee. I need my father's files back; I should have never relinquished them."

"Well, you know they're evidence now and that is not possible. Please, Libby, you need to do as I've already asked. Stay patient, keep an ultra-low profile right now. For the same reason we're concerned about your mother's safety. There are people who *will* retaliate. It'll all work out. Trust me." She hung up.

Frustrated, I slammed my fist against the countertop just as I heard the front door lock click. The doorknob twisted and in walked Greg. Tears welled and by the time I made it into his arms, they streamed down my face. He held me close and Shadow wound herself between our legs, trying to get his attention with her own love.

When I pulled away, I wiped my face and simply said, "We need to call the Johnsons over. It's time we put our heads together and finish this business once and for all."

No questions asked. He simply followed my lead.

CHAPTER THIRTY-SIX

As Detective Alvarez's words echoed in my mind—
"keep a low profile … retaliation"—I couldn't shake the
unease that had settled over me. Greg, Lexi, JJ, and I had
just finished discussing it around my kitchen table when
my phone vibrated with a new email notification.

Curious, I opened it, only to find a cryptic message
from an unknown sender: *"If you want the truth about your
father, meet me at the old train yard. Midnight. Alone."*

There were no identifying details, just the message
and a single attachment: a photo of my father standing
in front of the amethyst mine entrance, holding a bundle
of documents and speaking with none other than Peter
Daniels. The date on the photo was the week before my
father's death.

I held up my phone to show the others, and they stared, stunned. Greg was the first to break the silence. "Do you think it's real?"

My mind spun as I tried to recall why it seemed familiar. *Had I seen this photo before?*

JJ nodded toward the phone. "Whoever sent this knows something. They're definitely trying to expose Daniels, but what I'm more concerned about is that they may try to trap you."

"But why?" Lexi asked, looking around nervously. "They could have done that at the mine easily. If they meant business, that is."

Deciding, and not wanting to debate it any longer, I stood up. "I have to go. This might be the only way to find out what really happened to him."

Greg placed a hand on my shoulder. "Not alone, Libby. We all go together."

The group strategized, deciding that JJ would follow from a distance, staying hidden in case things went sideways. Greg insisted on accompanying me, just to keep an eye out for anything unexpected.

When midnight finally arrived, Greg and I pulled up near the old train yard in south Phoenix, a desolate, sprawling area bathed in shadows. The air was thick with tension, every creak and whisper amplifying the suspense. We spotted a faint figure standing under a broken light post, his back turned to us. My stomach tightened as I recognized Peter Daniels.

He turned slowly, his expression unreadable, hands clasped tightly in front of him. "Libby, you were supposed to have come alone! This is much bigger than you realize."

I stepped closer; my voice unwavering. "You owe me the truth. There's more than what you've already divulged."

Daniels hesitated; his face shadowed. "Your father was getting close to … well, uh, something that could've destroyed everything. The mine, the insurance company—it's a front. A front for laundering money, for hiding evidence."

Greg's hand tightened around mine. "We know most of that. But hiding what evidence?"

Daniels' eyes darted to the shadows, as if he expected someone to emerge at any moment. "Human remains. Those bones in the mine … they're *not* ancient. And your father was on the verge of proving their connection to the insurance firm's activities. They were scared, Libby. They *still are.*"

I felt a chill wash over me as I connected the pieces. "And you're still part of it, aren't you? The cover-up, the threats—you were part of silencing him."

Before he could respond, headlights flashed across the lot. Several thugs emerged, led by Detective Ross. My heart rate skyrocketed.

"Well, isn't this touching," Ross sneered. "Looks like we've got ourselves a little reunion. You just can't leave well enough alone, can you, *Libby*?"

Daniels took a step back, his face pale. "Libby, go. Now!"

But Ross had already pulled a gun. "No one's going anywhere." He raised it toward us. "You don't know what you're messing with."

In a split-second decision, Greg stepped in front, shielding me. "We're not backing down, Ross."

Just then, JJ burst out from behind a stack of crates, catching Ross off guard. JJ raised his own gun, and shouted, "Drop it, Ross! It's over! You know this won't make anything better."

The standoff escalated, as everyone waited for someone to make the next move. Ross's grip tightened, his face twisting with rage. His unflinching eyes penetrated JJ's. "You don't understand. If the truth comes out, we *all* lose, you idiot!"

Daniels looked at me one last time, desperation in his eyes. "It's not just your father's death, Libby. It's ... *all of them.*"

With that, he turned and bolted into the shadows, Ross firing after him. Greg pulled me behind a stack of crates, crouching low, shielding me as the scene erupted in chaos. JJ took cover as well, and I realized we'd lost sight of Daniels when he sprinted away.

Ross cursed loudly, quickly calling on his mob to pursue. "Fan out—find Daniels! We're not losing him again!" he barked, sending his goons running toward the yard's perimeter, guns drawn.

JJ motioned for Greg and me to stay put, his face tense. "Let's wait till they're a safe distance off. If we can stay hidden, maybe we can get out of here without them noticing."

My head spun, processing Daniels' cryptic warning about my father's death being linked to *others*. I couldn't help but feel that Daniels had been on the verge of revealing something monumental. *What did he mean by 'all of them'? And who were the others?*

As we crouched in silence, I heard footsteps approaching—heavy, purposeful steps. We barely dared to breathe. I could feel Greg's hand on mine, his grip reassuring but tense. I peered around the crates and spotted Ross approaching, looking angrier than ever.

But he wasn't alone. Detective Alvarez appeared from the shadows; her expression conflicted as she stopped in front of Ross. My breath caught. Alvarez was supposed to be *our* ally, someone who'd been warning us to stay safe. Now she was standing beside Ross, his demeanor wavering.

"Is this really necessary, Ross?" Alvarez's voice was low, but her tone edged with doubt. "Daniels has already fled, and dragging innocent people into this—"

"Innocent?" Ross cut her off with a sneer. "They're meddling where they shouldn't. If Daniels gets to them, this whole operation's exposed."

I exchanged a shocked look with Greg. *Alvarez knew.* She'd known about the cover-up, the shady deals tied to the mine, and maybe even about my father's death. JJ's face hardened, the betrayal registering as he leaned closer to whisper, "So much for allies."

Alvarez shifted, casting a quick look over her shoulder. "Ross, we can't keep burying your messes. It's already caught up to you—and I'm not going down for this."

Ross looked furious. "And what? Let Daniels spill everything he knows? You have all the evidence in your possession now; *we're* not going down, Alvarez."

I could barely believe what I was hearing. The stakes were higher than I'd realized. It wasn't just my father's death or the mine's hidden secrets—this was a full-blown operation, with dirty cops and possibly even more deaths tied up in it.

After a tense pause, Alvarez finally stepped back, her face twisted in reluctant acceptance. "Fine," she muttered. "But this better be the last time we deal with Daniels. And listen, *I* deal with Libby and her friends—they'll stay quiet, I'll see to that."

Ross nodded, signaling for his men to regroup. "Agreed. No more loose ends."

Once they were long gone, JJ motioned for us to move, whispering urgently, "Let's get out of here now."

We quietly made our way back to our car parked discreetly several blocks away. I could barely contain the questions bubbling up inside as we reached safety.

"They're not just covering up my father's death. Ross, Alvarez, Daniels—there's no telling how many people are involved. And I think this proves it, JJ. Alvarez is the one in the department who is causing problems for you."

JJ nodded in agreement. "Now that we know just how far this goes, we can't trust *anyone* at the station. But if Daniels has more evidence, that could be our best shot."

I took a deep breath, gathering myself. How was I going to face Alvarez? Or how do we find Daniels now? I needed more answers from him. I was more than prepared to see this through, for my father, for myself, and for everyone who'd been hurt, or silenced, by these people. Then a horrible thought occurred to me. *Was Nathan one of those whom they've already silenced?*

CHAPTER THIRTY-SEVEN

The air inside my mother's home felt heavier than before she'd left for Colorado. I held the flashlight up to Greg at the top of the ladder, where he reached up to the attic's opening. Dust clouded the air as he lifted the lid, and then he disappeared inside.

"Got something," Greg's voice echoed from inside, his voice low, almost reverent. "You were right. There's more up here. I don't know why we hadn't checked earlier."

JJ stepped forward, his gaze now at the open hole in the ceiling. He took a few steps up the ladder. "Ready when you are!"

Greg appeared at the opening with the first box. JJ climbed one more rung and reached up. "Careful."

JJ stepped down a couple steps and twisted toward me.

"It's not too heavy."

I took the box from him and then handed it off to Lexi, who stacked the boxes in the living room. We repeated this until the attic was cleared.

After sorting boxes that were obviously filled with family belongings from those that appeared to be business related, we finally sat on the floor and began rifling through them. Hours later, when we were close to giving up, the energy in the room shifted.

Shadow barked and nudged JJ's arm when he opened the next box in front of him. Her nose knocked off the lid which was loosely in place. JJ looked inside, after quizzically eyeing the Labrador.

"This looks like a ledger," JJ muttered, flipping through pages filled with carefully handwritten notes. He paused, squinting at the faded ink, and then he gave another confused look toward Shadow, who sat there staring at him with intensity. "These are insurance claim payouts. Look here—names, dates, amounts … and most are flagged with some kind of code."

I leaned over his shoulder, my breath catching as I spotted my father's name. Shadow rested her head on my lap, obviously satisfied that we'd finally opened the correct box.

"That's … that's my dad. Right there." My voice cracked as I pointed out the entry with a trembling finger.

CLAIM: WORKPLACE ACCIDENT — $250,000 — DECEASED

Next to it, a faint mark, a symbol I didn't recognize.

"It's all here," JJ said grimly. "Look—Nathan Pierce was funneling money through fake claims. The names marked with this symbol—" he tapped the page, "—are probably the ones who didn't survive."

"Nathan?" My knees wobbled as I tried to stand. Greg quickly steadied me. "He *killed* them?" I whispered. "Including my dad?"

JJ nodded; his jaw tight. "Your father must've uncovered this. That's why he became a target. But there's more going on here. These payouts … they don't stop at Nathan."

He flipped to the back of the ledger, revealing a list of initials and corresponding amounts. "R.A. and A.R.," JJ read aloud. "Renee Alvarez and Alan Ross. They were taking cuts."

My head spun. Nathan Pierce? The *private investigator* who I'd hired to look into my father's death? The one who brought me to trust Renee Alvarez? *What in the devil…*

"JJ was right, this goes way higher than we thought," Greg said, his face pale. "Of course, we'd figured out Detective Ross, a trusted member of the police force. Now I think the question is: who are Nathan and Renee? Obviously, not who they said they were."

JJ pulled out his phone, snapping pictures of the ledger. "We need to get this to someone we can trust in the department. But we're not done yet."

Shadow let out a low growl, drawing their attention back to the hallway. The dog sniffed the air, her body tense.

"What is it, girl?" I asked, kneeling beside her.

Shadow ran to the ladder; we followed, our eyes staring up at the opening to the attic. "There's something else up there."

Greg squeezed through the opening again. Shadow let out a chipper bark this time—happy we understood her.

He shouted back through the opening, "There are several items laying around—a tattered jacket, a hard hat, and a sealed envelope."

I climbed several steps and plucked the envelope from his hands. The name scrawled across the front made my stomach churn: **Peter Daniels**. I fumbled and dropped it to the ground.

JJ bent over and retrieved it. He opened it carefully, revealing a handwritten letter. Reading, his voice wavered:

"To whoever finds this: If you're reading this, it means I couldn't stop them. Nathan Pierce and his people are dangerous. They're covering up deaths and laundering money through fraudulent claims. Leon Madsen tried to warn us, but now they're coming for both of us. I'm sorry for the lives lost because of my silence. I hope this evidence is enough to stop them. — Peter Daniels"

Greg clenched his fists. "So, Peter wasn't innocent, but at least at some point, he tried to do the right thing."

My jaw clenched. "Then why hadn't he given this over to the authorities? He put on an entire front for *me*, when Nathan and I came to his office. The encounter at the mine…"

Before anyone could respond, my phone buzzed. I glanced at the screen; my eyes flew open. I'd missed several calls from my mother.

"It's Mom, trying to get a hold of me. Now she's texted: Someone delivered a note to the Lawson house with my name on it. It only said 'You're next."

JJ paled. "Nathan. He's after her. If Nathan knows about the investment fund, he'll do whatever it takes to silence her."

My hands balled into fists. "Renee told him where she is! We've got to stop them."

Shadow barked, the sound sharp, as if she understood the gravity of the moment. The rest of us exchanged a glance.

* * *

We scrambled to make plans. I had to get to my mom as soon as possible.

JJ assured us he'd contact the local police in Pagosa Springs, Colorado. They'd monitor the Lawson place. Meanwhile, Greg and I hurriedly packed my 4Runner, and filled it with gas.

Shadow hopped in and within the hour, we set out on the road trip—I-17 to I-40 and then on to Gallup, New Mexico. We had JJ on the phone, working through how we set the trap. Despite all the evidence we'd collected to this point, it would be sweet if we could wrangle a confession.

Taking turns driving, we navigated the highways through Arizona, New Mexico, and into Colorado, finally making it to the Lawson ranch west of Pagosa Springs nearly ten hours later.

CHAPTER THIRTY-EIGHT

The Lawson's home sat nestled among towering pines, its rustic charm masking the tension that gripped its occupants. Snow fell in thick, silent flakes, muffling the outside world. Inside, my mom paced the length of the small living room, her hands wringing together.

"He's out there, Libby. I can feel it." Mom's voice sounded drained as they sat waiting.

I reached for my mother's hands. "It's okay, Mom. The police are involved and they'll keep us safe."

Greg, crouched near the window, peered into the darkened forest with binoculars. "The snow is picking up. If Nathan's coming, he'll use the cover of night. I'm glad we got my parents over to their friend's house earlier."

"Yeah. That's great, but I'm still not comfortable using

my mom as a pawn."

"I know, hon. But this plan is going to work—and we'll keep Julia out of harm's way."

Shadow stood alert by the door, her ears twitching at every creak the home made. The dog's presence was a comfort, but even so, the tension in the room was palpable.

A faint thud came from the back of the house. Everyone froze.

Greg motioned for silence, holding up his hand. He crept toward the sound; Shadow and I followed close behind. Julia stayed rooted in place, clutching a fireplace poker as if it were a lifeline.

Greg opened the back door cautiously, the icy wind rushing in. The disturbed snow was immediately apparent; fresh footprints led from the edge of the tree line to the back porch.

"He's been here," Greg whispered.

A flicker of movement in the woods caught Shadow's attention. Her low growl in her throat was the warning, then she bolted outside, barking furiously.

"Shadow, no!" I called, but she was already out of sight.

Greg grabbed a flashlight and gave me a stern look. "Well, he knows we're here now. Stay here and lock the door!"

He plunged out into the cold, following Shadow's barks. The snow muffled his footsteps, but through the window, I saw his breath come out in sharp puffs, visible in the flashlight's beam.

"Shadow!" he called again, his voice echoing through the trees.

A human cry rang out, followed by Shadow's bark. Greg aimed the flashlight toward the sound, illuminating a tall figure struggling to fend off the large black dog.

"Nathan," Greg said in a gruff tone.

Nathan Pierce turned; his face twisted in anger. He held a crowbar in one hand, the other raised defensively as Shadow lunged again. "Call off the mutt, or she's dead!"

"Shadow, heel!" Greg commanded. She obeyed reluctantly, retreating to his side but keeping her eyes locked on Nathan.

Nathan straightened; his brow furrowed as he recognized Greg. They both turned when they saw me running toward them. Nathan lifted the crowbar and Shadow lunged once again.

Greg yelled, "Shadow, heel!" Then he held a hand up to stop me from coming closer. Shadow ran for me and heeled right on my foot.

Nathan snarled at me. "You should've stayed out of this, little girl."

I stepped forward, my fear overshadowed by rage. "I can't believe you, Nathan. Why? I trusted you—and you've lied to me all this time. You lied to my father!" Then the worst thought crept in. "*You* killed my father!"

He let out a maniacal laugh. "Your father couldn't leave well enough alone. He thought he could expose everything, but all he did was dig his own grave. Same as you're doing right now," he hissed.

I hoped the cops nearby were getting all this.

"How'd you do it, Nathan?"

"Do what? Your father died of a heart attack, plain and simple. You cannot prove otherwise."

"How'd you get him to trust you?"

"Oh, that. Easy—you Madsens are *so gullible*."

His evil tone gave me more goosebumps than the

winter's chill. "If you wanted to get rid of us, why not do it sooner? Why pretend all this time you were helping me? I mean, if I was such an easy mark..."

"The plan was to obtain all the evidence you possessed. As naïve as you Madsens are, your tenaciousness is much stronger. You were supposed to have handed everything over to us and dropped it." He thrust forward, trying to grab for me.

Greg moved to block Nathan's path. "You're not walking out of here. We have the ledger, your cohorts have turned on you, it's over, Nathan."

Nathan laughed, a hollow, chilling sound. "You think Ross and Alvarez will let this go public? They own half the department. By the time your *so-called evidence* sees the light of day, you'll all be long gone. I'm not the only one who can make people disappear."

My eyes blazed. "You're done, Nathan. We have much more than what we handed over to you as our *private investigator*. You're finished, you *fraud*."

Nathan's smirk faltered for a split second, but he recovered quickly, tightening his grip on the crowbar. "Then I've got nothing to lose."

He lunged at Greg, but Shadow reacted faster, barreling into Nathan's mid-section and knocking him off balance. The crowbar fell into the snow as Nathan scrambled to his feet, clambering to find it.

Greg was on him in an instant, pinning him up against a tree. "It's over!" Greg growled.

Nathan struggled, his breath coming in ragged gasps. "You have no idea who you're dealing with!"

A burst of light flooded the scene as red and blue strobes reflected off the snow. Sirens shrieked, piercing the once quiet night.

JJ emerged from one of the squad cars and ran toward us, gun drawn. "Nathan Pierce, you're under arrest!"

Nathan's defiance crumbled as officers swarmed the area, securing him in handcuffs. Greg and I stared with confusion as JJ approached us.

"Nice work," JJ said, patting Greg on the shoulder. He turned to me. "You okay?"

I nodded, though my body still trembled. "I thought you were going to let local law enforcement handle it. You followed us to Colorado?"

JJ nodded with a wide smile on his face.

I hugged my friend. "Did you guys get it all?" I asked, pulling the earpiece out, then unzipping my jacket and awkwardly reaching under my clothing to pull the surveillance wiring off my body. I handed the jumble of wires and electronics over to him.

"Sure did—that was great."

"We still need Ross and Alvarez."

JJ's jaw tightened. "I know. Don't worry, we've got their trail. And this guy will help us bring them down, whether he realizes that right now." He tilted his head toward Nathan, who was being carted off by an officer.

As they led Nathan away, I saw Mom step out onto the porch. She locked eyes with us, looking distraught. Worried, I ran to her side.

"It's over, Mom," I said, wrapping my arms around her. "No one will hurt us."

Mom clung to me, tears streaming down her face. "I was so afraid I'd lose you, too."

Greg walked over and placed a reassuring hand on my back and wrapped his arms around both of us, his voice soft. "You didn't. We're all safe now."

Shadow barked triumphantly, her tail wagging as if to declare victory.

But even as relief settled over us, I knew there was more to do. Nathan was in custody, but Ross and Alvarez were still out there somewhere. And even though it appeared that Peter Daniels would cooperate, he wasn't in custody yet. We wouldn't stop until they paid for their crimes.

JJ walked up to us just as his phone buzzed with a new message. The sender was anonymous, but the words sent a chill down my spine: You've only scratched the surface.

CHAPTER THIRTY-NINE

Back in Arizona, the tension in JJ's home office was electric as he paced back and forth, his phone clutched tightly in one hand. Greg, Lexi, and I sat around the desk, watching him. The anonymous message had rattled us all.

"This is it," JJ said, stopping to look at them. "We take down Ross and Alvarez, or they bury us along with the evidence."

My only consolation was that before Greg and I drove home from Colorado, we put Mom on a plane to Florida, where the Lawsons and their friends would look out for her. Five minutes ago, she sent me a photo of herself on a beach with a smile and an umbrella drink. I forwarded it to Jordan, in hopes that her relentless calls would cease.

Now, JJ leaned forward, his expression sharp. "We've

got the ledger, but we need more. Ross and Alvarez have too many allies in the department. If we don't tie this up perfectly, they'll walk."

Greg spoke up. "Nathan might be willing to help us. He knows how they operate, where the money goes. Like you said before, he might cooperate to save himself."

Then it occurred to me, and I interrupted. "Have they extradited him yet?"

JJ nodded, then sighed. "It's a risk, but it is worth trying. Let's see what we can do there. I think I know who I can trust in the department now, but I've really got to watch my back."

Lexi jumped up when she heard their son on the other side of the door. "Mom!" She left to go tuck him back into bed.

Greg, JJ, and I worked out the next day's plan.

* * *

Nathan sat in the cold, sterile interrogation room, his cuffs clinking as he shifted uncomfortably. His defiance had dulled, replaced by a wary resignation. JJ entered the room with Detective Ross's name looming over them like a shadow. He knew he had limited time with this suspect before someone in the department leaked his movements.

"You want to get out of this alive?" JJ asked, dropping a thick file onto the table. "Then start talking. Ross and Alvarez are going down, and you're going to help us."

Nathan scoffed, his eyes impatiently cast upward. "Why should I? You're just going to lock me up either way."

JJ's voice cut through the tension. "Because if you don't, you'll take all the blame. And trust me, Ross and

Alvarez won't hesitate to let you rot while they enjoy the millions they've stolen."

Nathan's jaw tightened. A tough act, but the fear in his eyes was unmistakable. "They're not just stealing. They're killing anyone who gets in their way. You have no idea what they're capable of."

"Then help us stop them," JJ said. "Give us their locations, their contacts, anything we can use to bring them down."

Nathan hesitated. JJ opened the folder he brought in with him. Thumbing through the papers, he grunted, then looked at Nathan again and slowly shook his head.

"You know we have enough to put you away for a very long time." His fingers flipped through more paperwork, slowly and methodically. "We could work out a deal, though. I believe you got tied up in their scheme and they're going to let you take the fall. Am I right?"

Nathan's face remained motionless. Eyes straight ahead.

"Well, we can play it however you'd like. If you'd like to cooperate, I'll recommend a plea deal. If you don't start cooperating within the next few minutes, I'll walk out of here and we'll let the chips fall where they may. Your choice."

Slowly, Nathan turned his face toward JJ's. Staring intensely, he remained silent. Finally, a slight nod of his head. Then his eyes fixed on the table in front of him and quietly, he surrendered information. "Almost everything has already been transferred and hidden in the mine. However, there's a warehouse in downtown Phoenix. There may be more evidence there; I overheard Ross directing some of his thugs to get it cleared out."

That's all JJ needed for now. He glanced at the one-way mirror and gave a nod. Two officers entered the room and escorted Nathan back to his cell. Greg and I met JJ out in the hallway and he motioned to the rear exit doors.

As he held the door open for us, he simply stated, "Let's grab some lunch and talk elsewhere."

Over burgers and fries, he laid out a plan. He'd have to get others involved but was confident he could pull it off. He only needed a little more time.

"In the meantime, I want both of you to stay diligent. Libby, maybe you could pay Rob Turner a visit within the next few days. We need to learn more about that money your mom discovered—where did it come from? *Who* invested it in her name?"

"Sure, no problem."

Greg offered to set up some cameras around Julia's house, just in case. There was still concern that they'd break in there looking for more evidence.

"It's more probable that Alvarez and Ross are on the run—meaning, out of the state. Now, with Nathan's arrest, I'm sure they're worried he'll talk. Who knows how desperate they'll become? Let's take no chances."

* * *

The next evening, we got the word that the operation was going down. Under the cover of night, JJ led a SWAT team to the Phoenix location.

Despite JJ's initial protests, Greg, Lexi, and I waited safely, but anxiously, nearby. Shadow paced beside us, her ears perked for any sign of danger.

JJ's voice crackled through my earpiece he provided.

"We're going in. Stay put."

The sound of boots crunching on gravel filled my ears as the team approached the warehouse. JJ gave a signal, and we could hear the door being breached with a thunderous bang.

Inside, chaos erupted. The armed guards we'd been warned about opened fire, but the SWAT team was well-prepared. In the midst of the chaos, I heard JJ's shout: "Ross! Alvarez! Stop!"

Ross's voice growled, "You don't know what you're messing around with, JJ. This isn't just about us. You take us down, and the entire department crumbles."

"Then it crumbles," JJ said. "You're done."

The shot that rang out nearly deafened me through the earpiece. But then I clearly heard Alvarez's voice. "I'm not going to prison," she hissed.

"You should've thought about that before you killed innocent people," JJ said. Handcuffs clicked into place.

* * *

The teams JJ sent to the mining operation found loads of evidence. Even the warehouse still contained damning proof of their corroboration. Between both sites, all the remaining pieces of the puzzle were discovered: bank accounts, falsified reports, and proof of bribes paid to silence witnesses and investigators. For me, the saddest part was learning about the human remains that the forensics teams uncovered. These were sick people hellbent on money and power. The media caught wind of the scandal, and the fallout was immediate and widespread.

Prosecutors charged Ross and Alvarez with conspiracy,

fraud, and multiple counts of murder. The exposure of other corrupt officers unraveled their network, leading to a massive overhaul of the department.

Nathan Pierce, true to his word, cooperated fully, earning himself a reduced, but hefty sentencing. Regardless of what I thought of the man, he ultimately nailed one of Ross' goons as the one who poisoned my father, causing his heart attack. At least I had closure related to my father's death. The knowledge that the person responsible was held accountable helped, though it wouldn't bring Leon Madsen back.

Also, Rob Turner, and his college buddy, Tony Winder, were of great help. Both divulged their knowledge about the scheme. Poor Tony, truly he knew so little, but got caught up in it, anyway. Rob, as an investment banker, was in deep trouble with the feds—the U.S. Securities and Exchange Commission.

The one helpful bit of new information I learned was that the investment fund was legitimate and Rob was not involved at all. None of it had to do with the fallout from the insurance fraud, and my mom had been the beneficiary all along. Turns out, Dad had invested wisely, but at his death, no one in the family knew about the account to let the company know when he passed.

I learned that the three million dollars was Nathan's largest incentive and the major reason he agreed to work with me when I showed up at his office that day, asking for his help. Once he had learned from Rob that the Madsens held an account worth that much money, he was determined to get his hands on it. The ruse to get my mother isolated away from me in Colorado was all his idea. He hadn't counted on family being there to protect her.

It also came out in several depositions that none of them—Detective Ross, Renee Alvarez, Nathan Pierce, Peter Daniels—took me seriously when I began to look into my father's death. They thought all along they could string me along and play me and I'd give up.

That was their first and last mistake.

CHAPTER FORTY

G reg, Shadow, and I stood in the arrivals hall at Phoenix Sky Harbor Airport, scanning the crowd for our parents. It was late afternoon, and the winter sun was low on the horizon and casting a warm glow through the glass panels, adding a touch of brightness to the otherwise bustling terminal. Shadow, dressed in her service dog vest, sat obediently at my feet, tail wagging in anticipation. Her friendly demeanor drew smiles from passersby.

"There they are," Greg said, pointing down the long hallway. Julia, Anne, and Bill were walking toward us, pulling their luggage behind, their sun-kissed faces with relaxed expressions a testament to their time in Key West. Julia waved enthusiastically; her straw hat was slightly askew from the motion.

As they reached us, Anne embraced me first, clenching tight. "Oh, it's so good to see you, sweetheart," she said. "I hope everything is okay now?" she asked, pulling back to see my eyes. "You wouldn't believe how much we needed this trip; how much your mother needed the break."

"I know, I can see she looks so much more relaxed. And everything is all taken care of here," I replied, smiling as I took in Anne's vibrant floral blouse and Bill's relaxed khaki shorts. "You both look like you just stepped out of a travel magazine."

"We might have overdone the Key lime pie," Bill admitted with a chuckle, patting his stomach. "But it was worth every bite."

Julia knelt to greet Shadow, scratching behind her ears. "And how's my favorite grand-dog?" she cooed, earning a joyful bark from the Labrador. She stood and hugged Greg next. "Thanks for taking such good care of us … everything work out alright?"

He nodded. "I'm just glad you all had somewhere safe you could go. But you're not getting off that easily. We need to hear all the Key West stories."

As we walked toward the parking garage, the parents shared snippets of their adventures: snorkeling near the coral reefs, a sunset sail where dolphins played alongside the boat, and Julia's triumphant karaoke rendition of *Margaritaville* at a local bar. I couldn't help but laugh at the thought of my usually reserved mother letting loose onstage.

"And Anne here became quite the conch fritter connoisseur," Bill teased, earning an eye roll from his wife.

"They're not all created equal," Anne replied defensively. "But I'll admit, I'll miss the fresh seafood."

Once we reached the car, Greg loaded the suitcases

into the back of the 4Runner while I helped my mom get settled into the backseat with Shadow. As we pulled out of the airport, the conversation shifted to upcoming plans. We told them what we knew about the engagement party Lexi would soon be hosting.

"But first," Julia said with a contented sigh, "I just want to get home and sleep in *my own bed*."

"That's the best part of any trip, isn't it?" Greg agreed, glancing at me with a knowing smile.

The car filled with laughter and the warm chatter of family reconnecting, a welcome contrast to the chaos we had all faced in recent months. For now, life felt wonderfully ordinary, and that was more than enough.

* * *

Anne and Bill extended their stay with us by a few days, excited to attend the Valentine's Day engagement party hosted by Lexi and JJ. It was a much different visit than it had been when they were last here at Thanksgiving. First, with only the two of them, it was much more manageable for them to stay in our home with us. But, also, without Greg's siblings around, I had the opportunity to get to know his parents better.

They wanted to visit where their children had stayed in Greg's fifth-wheel out on his land near the Superstition Mountains, so we planned a late afternoon cookout on one of the days. As we watched the sunset on the mountain range, we found ourselves discussing future plans.

"Any chance I could convince you to move out here someday, Mrs. Lawson?" Greg asked me with a wide smile.

"I'm warming to the idea."

His parents' faces lit up. We talked hypothetically, each of us contributing our ideal dream home elements. At the end of it all, Greg and I really were on the same page with what we'd want in a home. I only had to wrap my head around not being walking distance from my work. We'd get there, though; I really loved this location and the five-acre property he owned was stunning.

His mother thought so too. "I can just see all the littles running around here one day."

My pulse quickened. *Littles? Like, she's counting on grandchildren?* Well, that's probably a conversation for another day.

* * *

Valentine's Day was never anything I'd actively celebrated before. This year, however, Lexi and JJ decorated their home with soft pink, white, and red decorations, creating a festive yet elegant atmosphere for our engagement party.

Sage, Bella, Brad, Cody, Kathleen, and Diane mingled with laughter and clinking glasses, while my mom and her dear friend, Maggie, sat together across the room. It sounded like they had much to catch up on after she'd been gone for several weeks. Jordan was there with her children: Apple, Annie, Ryan, and Chase. Along with Joshua and Shadow, they all ran around playing, adding a lively energy to the gathering.

Anne and Bill felt right at home among the group, having met everyone at Thanksgiving. I enjoyed watching them chatting with Brad and Cody about their latest travels and catching up with Maggie. Later in the evening, Greg and I spent time with Lexi and JJ, exchanging stories about the recent adventures and our plans for the future.

The highlight of the night came when Greg raised a toast to Lexi and JJ for their generous hosting. "Here's to love, family, and friends," he said, as his voice cracked, choked briefly with gratitude. "You all accepted me into Libby's circle and I'll never be able to express how much that means to me. We've had many great memories over the past year—or more? What it's been now?" he turned to me, asking.

"Nearly two years, sweetie."

He blushed. "I should have known that. Anyway, the time has gone so quickly. It seems like yesterday that I met you, Libby Madsen. That was the best day of my life. I still remember vividly—the campground; the s'mores party, and seeing you off in the distance admiring the sunset. You turned around and took my breath away. You still take my breath away every single time I look at you." His voice cracked again. "I look forward to spending every day of my life with you. And to many more celebrations like this with our friends." He lifted his glass of champagne.

Tears streamed down my face. I had no words and even if I did, I wouldn't be able to get them out. I raised my glass as cheers erupted, filling the room with clinking glasses and heartfelt smiles. He leaned over and our lips found one another's.

A few playful jeers, and then JJ shouted, "Get a room!" before we all broke out into laughter.

It was a night to remember, and as Anne and Bill prepared to leave the next morning, we couldn't help but feel grateful for the love that surrounded us.

EPILOGUE

Several months later, JJ stood on the steps of City Hall, surrounded by his family and colleagues. The mayor handed him a plaque, her voice filled with gratitude.

"For his bravery and integrity, Detective Jeff Johnson is awarded the Medal of Valor. His efforts have not only brought criminals to justice, but have restored faith in our law enforcement."

I clapped loudly, tears filled my eyes, and I was so proud of my dear friend. Shadow barked, tail wagging.

After the ceremony, JJ approached Greg and me. "We did it. And, I have you two to thank for this," he said, holding up his medal, his magnificent smile filling his face.

I nodded, my heart lighter than it had been in years. "We did. And my dad can finally rest in peace. Thank you for believing in the cause—and allowing us to stay involved. I know how hard that must have been for you."

"Well, don't go getting over confident, Miss Libby. You overstepped..." he stopped and smiled. His eyes sparkled with his typical friendly, teasing manner. "You're welcome, my friend. I'm impressed with your fortitude. You put many of our investigators to shame. Honestly, the way you dig right in ... you're relentless." He gave me a giant hug.

Greg agreed with JJ's praise. He put an arm around my shoulders, then turned his head to our friend. "What's next for you, JJ? Big promotion, I would imagine?"

JJ shrugged, humble as always. "Not really sure. There's still work to be done. But maybe we'll take a vacation first." He pulled Lexi in closer and gave her a big kiss.

Greg and I admired our dutiful friends and when they came up for air, we noticed JJ blushing. He reached down and picked up Joshua, raising him over his head and plopping him down on his shoulders, leaving the little man's legs dangling on either side.

Shadow whined, worming her way through all our legs, right into the middle of our group. Laughter took over and justice prevailed.

Author's Note

I hope you enjoyed this one. And thanks for your patience as we let Greg discover the exact right time and place to propose. Yes, it took several books before we got there, but each story was so much fun to write, watching him fussing about how to do it 'perfectly.' LOL! Now, I need to come up with *when* they're getting married and what mystery will surround their nuptials. Hmmm … any ideas? I'd love to hear from you.

I took a LOT of liberties with this story. For anyone living in the Phoenix area, especially the East Valley, you may be familiar with the Four Peaks Wilderness Area. There's so much outdoor recreation there—whether four-wheeling, hiking, horseback riding, etc. It's stunning country and everything outdoor enthusiasts love. What some may not know … yes, there really is an amethyst mine!

I attended a lecture at the Superstition Mountain Museum during February, 2022, which inspired me to write this book. My husband, mother-in-law, and I, along with dozens of others, listened to the owner of the amethyst mine narrate the history behind his operation. I did not know, until that day, that Arizona had an amethyst mine—it was fascinating! And, of course, the entire time we sat there, a story was forming in my mind—I just *knew* I had to write a mystery surrounding amethysts.

And that's about where reality ends. Absolutely *nothing* is real in this book. The settings, characters, and crimes are all completely made up. Oh, and, it's nothing like what I imagined the story to be that day, sitting out in the warm sunshine in the shadows of the Superstition mountains listening to that lecture. Somehow, this story just took on a life of its own. All I knew for sure was that Libby, Greg, and Shadow would hike Four Peaks. I knew it had to be adventurous, magical, and somehow Greg would propose in this tenth Libby Madsen story. How the rest came to be happened one page at a time.

Hope you enjoyed it!
Jennifer

What's next for Libby and Shadow?
We may be hearing wedding bells … unless a new
mystery gets in the way. Only time, and the imagination
of award-winning author Jennifer J. Morgan, will tell!

**Watch for Book 11 in this "impressively original
and deftly crafted"* series!**
*Midwest Book Review

* * *

Thank you for taking the time to read *Ghostly Amethyst
Shadows*. If you enjoyed it please tell your friends, and
I would be so grateful if you would consider posting a
review.
Word of mouth is an author's best friend, and very
much appreciated.
Thank you,
Jennifer Morgan

* * *

**Get another free book from Jennifer—scan the
QR code to find out how!**

Books in the Libby Madsen Cozy Mysteries series:

Let's connect!

Website: jenniferjmorgan.com
Email: jennifer@jenniferjmorgan.com
Facebook: facebook.com/profile.
php?id=100076154359528
Twitter: twitter.com/JenniferJMorga3
BookBub: bookbub.com/profile/433830544
Goodreads: goodreads.com/user/show/148099219-
jennifer-morgan

About the Author

Jennifer grew up in the desert Southwest where she always dreamed of becoming an author. When she was younger, she was a huge fan of suspense/thriller novels—favorites being Dean Koontz, Stephen King, and James Patterson. Cozy mystery is more of a favorite today—enjoying the fun and adventurous spirit of authors such as Kathi Daley, Tanya Kappes, Joanne Fluke, and of course, Connie Shelton.

Jennifer is a member of Sisters in Crime - National, and the Desert Sleuths Chapter in Arizona.

When she's not writing, Jennifer enjoys camping, hiking, and traveling with her husband and two dogs. She also enjoys arts and crafts, always taking on a new project that sparks her creativity. You'll find all these passions featured in her Libby Madsen Cozy Mystery series.